Aubrey Menen was born in 1912 i_
parentage, and was educated at Uni
worked at several jobs at various times he was a drama critic,
stage director, press officer, scriptwriter, education officer for
the Government of India and head of the Motion Picture
Department for the J. Walter Thompson Company, London—
before turning to writing full time. In the course of a long writing
career he published several well received novels including *The
Prevalence of Witches* (1947), *The Stumbling Stone* (1949), *The
Backward Bride* (1950), *The Duke of Gallodoro* (1952), *SheLa*
(1962) and *A Conspiracy of Women* (1966). He also wrote a
number of non-fiction books and an autobiography *The Space
Within the Heart* (1970). His book *Four Days of Naples* (1979) is
to be filmed in Hollywood and his satirical *Rama Retold* (1954) is
being prepared for Broadway. Aubrey Menen died in Trivan-
drum in 1989.

Aubrey Menen
The Abode of Love

*The conception, financing and daily routine of
an English Harem in the middle of the
nineteenth century described in
the form of a novel*

PENGUIN BOOKS

Penguin Books (India) Ltd, 72-B, Himalaya House
23 Kasturba Gandhi Marg, New Delhi-110 001. India
Penguin Books Ltd, Harmondsworth, Middlesex, England
Viking Penguin Inc, 40 West 23rd Street, New York, N.Y. 10010, U.S.A.
Penguin Books Australia Ltd, Ringwood, Victoria, Australia
Penguin Books Canada Ltd. 2801 John Street, Markham, Ontario, Canada L3R1B4
Penguin Books (N.Z.) Ltd, 182-190 Wairau Road, Auckland 10, New Zealand

First Published by Scribners 1956
Published in Penguin Books 1973
Reprinted 1989
Reissued in Penguin Books India 1989
Copyright © The Estate of Aubrey Menen 1988, 1989

Made and printed in India by Ananda Offset Pvt. Ltd.

For
Philip Dallas

Note

Readers will wish to know if the principal characters of this book ever existed. They did. Henry James Prince, the five Nottidge sisters, Josiah, the four Lampeter Brethren and Julia were all real persons, some of whom lived and died in the Abode of Love, which was a real place.

I have based this narrative on W. Hepworth Dixon's contemporary report of his visit to the Abode, which will be found in his book *Spiritual Wives.**

Henry James Prince died in 1899. The Abode was subsequently revived by a self-styled follower of his. But I am not concerned, in this story, with that revival, either directly or by implication.

A.M.

*Tauchnitz Collection of British Authors, Leipzig 1868, 2 Vols.

Contents

Henry James Prince

IN 1851 the founder of the Abode of Love made one of his rare appearances in public. He went up to London in the company of three of his wives to see the Great Exhibition. He did the trip like a gentleman, driving round Hyde Park in a splendid carriage, with postillions. The postillions wore no hats. When they were asked why, they replied that they did it out of respect for the sacred character of their master who was Mr Prince of Spaxton, in Somerset.

When this singular man returned to his house, the coach was driven through an open gate, then up a broad drive, past a church with an unfinished tower, and so to the door of a large house that was joined to the church as though it were a rectory. The house, however, did not look like a rectory because it was much too large and splendid.

As the coach drew up, the door was opened, footmen came out, and behind them a major-domo, a butler and then maids, correctly starched and smiling. Prince and his wives dismounted, and went into the house. Here Prince was affectionately greeted by two more women, who were also his wives, and several men. Kisses and handshakes were exchanged, and then the travellers went to their rooms. A little later they came down again, refreshed and in a change of clothes. Then Prince, his five wives, and the attendant gentlemen all went in to tea.

They did not, however, go into the drawing-room. Instead, they turned off from the hallway and went through a corridor. At the end of this corridor was a doorway of gothic design. Opening this they went into the church. Once in the church, they did not go down on their knees to give thanks for a happy trip. They joined some companions round a large fireplace in which a log fire was burning, and, amid a great deal of cheerful gossiping, ate anchovy sandwiches, watercress sandwiches, and crumpets.

It must not be imagined that they did this while they sat in the pews. There were no pews. Instead there were comfortable armchairs, and a couch. The windows were of stained glass, as is proper for a church, but the evening light shone down through prophets, saints and angels, on to a red turkey carpet, at the corners of which were fashionably set out some potted palms. There was also a billiard table, but this was not in use because everybody was too busy either eating crumpets or asking questions about the Great Exhibition, or answering them.

Who was the master of this enviable house, this strange church, and five wives? He was an ex-curate. Some years before he had taken up his post in a village nearby, full of noble intentions. In a short time, his flock had driven him out for praying too much, and for kissing his female parishioners. He had left, and after experiencing some remarkable changes of fortune, he had returned, triumphantly, with a harem of wives and a body of faithful disciples. I shall now tell how and why he did it.

*

Henry James Prince was born in 1811, and spent his childhood at No. 5 Widcombe Crescent, Bath, with his mother, who let rooms. He was a sickly child with a perennially upset stomach who spent a good deal of his time in the local church. This suggested to everyone who knew him that he would grow up to be a clergyman, except to his mother, who, in the mysterious manner of determined mothers, was convinced that it showed that he wanted to be a doctor. He took his degree at Apothecary's Hall and actually practised for three years, to his mother's great content, since she had always wanted a doctor in the family. But he fell sick; he fell so sick that he could no longer practise as a doctor. Thus he found himself with nothing to do, and no money except his mother's small profits from her boarding-house.

He got better in health but not in his prospects. The only employment that he had was to read aloud to an elderly woman who had inherited some money and who now lodged with his mother. Her favourite book in the Bible was the Song of Songs, or as it is also known, the Song of Solomon. One day when Prince was reading aloud a particularly amorous passage, the elderly lady burst into tears, flung herself on Prince's breast and declared that she loved him.

In this way Henry James Prince learned of his two great gifts, about which he had not known before. These were the great attraction that he exercised for women of all ages, and secondly, his beautiful speaking voice. He was a handsome man. He had soft grey eyes, abundant and silky hair, a wan, but not too wan, cheek and well-shaped lips. His figure was slender but harmonious and he had small feet. All these advantages paled beside his voice, which was quiet and – to a woman – thrilling. This soothing yet magnetic voice remained with him until he died, and its effect on women was something akin to the purring of a tiger which is said so to confuse the tiger's prey that it walks straight into his mouth.

The elderly lady now told Prince that she was willing to do anything that he wanted. He asked for time to think, was granted it, and then announced that what he wanted most of all was to be sent to a theological college so that he could become a clergyman. The elderly lady praised so pious an intention, and gave him the money to pay his fees. Prince, in gratitude, married her, but since she died shortly afterwards she is not numbered among the wives that he subsequently kept in his harem.

Prince's choice of a career was no doubt sincere, but it was also practical. For a man with good looks and a fine speaking voice the pulpit was, in those days, the best platform on which to perform. It may be said that it was the only platform, since the stage was in disrepute. Prince knew this, but it must not be supposed that he took his religion lightly. He took it very seriously indeed. He got himself enrolled in the Theological College at Lampeter, an easy-going institution that trained men for the equally easy-going Established Church, and in no time at all he had turned the place upside down.

He did this by insisting that the students, and the Principal of a theological college, even in England, should act as though Christianity was a serious religion, in which they truly believed. He began to gather the more impressionable students together in special and prolonged prayer meetings. These meetings were, at first, held in the privacy of his room. They could not be stopped by the authorities, since they were not against the letter of the rules of the college, however much they were against the spirit of the place. But then Prince began being a Christian outside his room, and particularly at the Principal's table. This brought him into bad odour. The Principal, the Reverend Alfred Ollivant, had been promoted in the Church and generously gave a dinner-party to the students to celebrate the fact. The bottle was being pushed round the table, and a toast was being proposed, when Prince rose. Prince objected. He said that they should rather as Christians fall on their knees and pray for Ollivant's soul. He then abruptly left the room.

At that time it was not the custom for clerical gentlemen to fall on their knees while at table; the most that was expected of them was that they should slide, quietly, under it: and it is never wise, at any time, to pray publicly for the soul of an established theologian. Prince became very unpopular, except with the group of young men he had gathered round himself.

These formed a prayerful company who called themselves, to the intense irritation of the Principal, the Lampeter Brethren. These young men met regularly to examine their consciences, pray together, encourage one another to wrestle with the devil, and to do all those things, in a word, that intense young men are wont to do, until they marry and their wives put their foot down. But there was this difference. When these young men married, their wives did not put their foot down. They all lived happily together in the Abode of Love.

But that came later. Meantime Prince was given his degree as a Doctor of Divinity, not with any warmth, but rather because it would have looked somewhat odd to have withheld it on the grounds that he was given to praying for people's souls. From much the same dilemma came the offer of a curacy, but it was one so tucked away in the countryside that it did not seem likely that Prince would be able to cause much trouble. It may be assumed that Prince knew better. He flung himself into his curacy with burning zeal and in no time at all he had saved the soul of the Rector.

This was the Reverend Samuel Starky. For those who do not know the intricacies of organization in the Anglican Church, it may be useful to say that the Rector was Prince's immediate (and emphatic) superior. Curates do not usually aspire to save their Rector's soul, and Rectors have sometimes been known to doubt if curates have got one. But Prince's feat was even more remarkable, since Starky was the son of Lady Mary Alicia Coventry and through her was connected with half the aristocracy of England. He was in every way a startling catch.

After this spiritual triumph, Prince was tempted, and unfortunately, he fell. Some of the women of the congregation asked the handsome and now celebrated curate to hold special prayer meetings for ladies only. He agreed. He prayed; they followed him. He went on to give readings from the Song of Songs, and immediately the little village of Charlinch was in an uproar. While he had been surrounded by theological students Prince had not strayed from the thorny path of religious devotion. But now he was surrounded by the adoration of farmers' wives, farmers' daughters, and the womenfolk of all ages from the nearby country houses. Unable to resist their charms, he kissed them. He was accused by husbands and brothers of doing worse. The women, embattled on behalf of their curate, denied the accusations, but, as is the way with women in romantic matters that concern them nearly, their denials were tantalizingly ambiguous.

Prince continued to read aloud from the Song of Solomon and the men of Charlinch took its pacific verses as an impudent declaration of war. Farmers and squires forbad their wives to go to church; wives burst into tears and called down imprecations drawn from the Bible on their husbands' ungodly heads. While Prince and Starky prayerfully vested in the vestry on Sunday mornings, in the village itself, doors slammed, crockery was broken, and scriptural shrieks and angry bellows destroyed what should have been the Sabbath calm. The farm labourers, not knowing whether to side with God or their employers, stood round in the churchyard, and hooted neutrally. The thing was a scandal. The Bishop came down to Charlinch from his palace in Wells and stilled the riot.

But he did not still Prince. The Bishop asked Prince, politely enough, to go to some other diocese and promised warmly to help him do so. This solution might not have looked entirely satisfactory from the overall view of, say, the Archbishop of Canterbury, but it looked excellent to the Bishop of Bath and Wells. Prince refused. The Bishop sighed, and kicked him out of his post.

Another bishop, His Grace Dr Allen, the Bishop of Ely, took the young man on in what seems to have been a spirit of Christian bravado. He gave him a curacy at Stoke, and in some forty months Prince had caused an uproar in Stoke that surpassed even that at Charlinch. The Bishop of Ely reluctantly agreed that the Bishop of Bath and Wells had known what he was talking about, and followed his example. Prince was kicked out of Stoke, and, as it so happened, out of the pale of the Christian Church. For Prince, on the recommendation of having been twice sacked from a curacy, now decided to hire a hall and make it a church of his own.

*

In the middle of all the hullabaloo, the kissing and the dismissals, the sister of the Reverend Starky had quietly fallen in love with Prince and made up her mind to marry him. Her name was Julia, and she was considered a beautiful woman at a time when the standards of beauty among Englishwomen were very high. She had the oval face and the level brows that were so much admired in those days, and large, tranquil eyes of the sort that, later, the pre-Raphaelite painters were to make famous. She was well-born, and showed it in her manner. She was, however, not rich, having only a tiny income of eighty pounds a year.

Her love for Prince had nothing to do with the Song of Songs or with religion in any shape or form. She loved him as any woman might love any man: and she loved him very dearly until the day of her death. She was, perhaps, the one true and good thing that came the way of Henry James Prince in his whole life. It would seem absurd, in view of his later actions, to say that he recognized this, but it is true. With others, Prince was often vain and egotistical in his behaviour. With Julia he was sane, self-critical, and sceptical about his pretensions. He was aware that she loved him for himself, and he showed to her, as he showed to very few other people, what his true self was like. This true self justified, in Julia's eyes, her love for him.

They married, and with the money which she brought him Prince hired a meeting-hall in Brighton and took lodgings across the road. He called the hall 'The Adullam' after the cave in which the unfortunate, the outcast and the desperate took shelter at David's summons. He, too, sent out a summons, to the Lampeter Brethren. They were by no means outcasts; several of them had landed posts as curates, but they came whenever their other duties allowed. So, of course, did the usual band of devoted women, and Prince launched a series of discourses, partly based on the wrath to come, a favourite topic of the times, and partly based, inevitably, on the Song of Songs.

*

At first the meetings were successful. But soon, with the coming of winter and the end of the Brighton season, his audience dwindled. The Lampeter Brethren found less and less time to spare from their duties, the women went back to London and their homes. Some evenings, especially during the dreary weeks of November, there was no one at all.

This failure was bitter, and Prince, tired in spirit after so many defeats and so much contumely, began to lose faith in himself.

One evening, when the rain beat incessantly on the windows, and nobody at all had come, Prince and Julia and the caretaker, a woman called Mrs Cusack and one of Mr Prince's admirers, were all three gathered round the stove at the gallery end of the hall, when a middle-aged man came in. He threw off his great-coat, and approached Prince. He asked if he might have a word in private with him. Mrs Cusack immediately took Julia away to her kitchen where she habitually made little suppers for them both, and Prince asked the man to draw a chair up to the stove, and to sit down.

The man explained that he was a humble follower of Prince's, an ex-sergeant of Her Majesty's Marines, who had attended all of Prince's meetings whenever he could. Prince, studying his features, recognized him as an obscure listener who always sat in the back row, even when there were not a dozen people sitting in the others. Prince put more coal on the stove, and invited the visitor to speak his mind.

The man thanked him, and said that he had had a misfortune. He would like to tell it to Prince. Prince nodded, but could scarcely suppress a sigh, for he felt that he already had more than his share of his own misfortunes. But in a few moments he was listening willingly, for Sergeant Matthew Bunt's story took him agreeably away from the hall, the rain, and his failure, to the sunshine of the mid-Pacific.

It also (though he did not know this as yet) marked the turning point of his life.

2

The Disgraceful Castaway

MATTHEW BUNT had joined the Marines at the age of thirteen and he had risen to be a sergeant. His promotion took place in the thirty-eighth year of his life. In the December of that year the ship in which he was sailing in the way of duty encountered a storm while some sixty leagues off the Marshall Islands. The storm, which began at six in the evening, increased in violence until midnight, when the ship struck. It was almost immediately dismasted, and her commander, judging that her situation was hopeless, gave the order to abandon ship.

This was done in as disciplined a manner as the tempest would allow, and although one boat was lost in the launching, with its complement, the others got away safely. But Matthew Bunt, while marshalling his men upon the sloping deck, slipped, and struck his head against a stanchion. The position in which he lay suggested to his comrades, who saw him only by the occasional glare of lightning, that he had broken his neck and was dead. In obedience to the commander's orders, he was left behind, there being no way of getting his insensible body into the already crowded boats.

But Matthew Bunt was not dead. He came to at six o'clock in the morning to find the storm abated and himself alone. He refreshed himself with some brandy which he found in a cabin, and, much restored, saw that the rock on which the ship had struck lay within a mile of a small island. While he was observing this, the ship settled, suddenly heeling over still farther and sending Bunt sliding down the deck. Thus warned of the danger in which he stood, he stripped himself to his drawers and immediately made his way down the side of the ship to clear water, into which he plunged and swam, without any great difficulty, to the shore.

The island was well wooded, but a promontory near the

beach gave Bunt a clear view over the whole of it. It was little more than a mile across, and Matthew Bunt saw with relief that there were some grass huts lining the shore of an adjacent bay. But these turned out to be deserted. The huts were empty save for a few large cooking pots and similar household objects too big to carry away. The native inhabitants, it would seem, had abandoned their village, but for what cause Bunt was quite unable to make out. Small patches of simply cultivated ground still bore fruits and edible tubers. Matthew Bunt made a meal of these, and consoled himself with the thought that the natives would return.

Two years later they had not done so, nor had the island been sighted by any ship. Meanwhile Matthew Bunt had found the climate equable, if rainy at certain seasons, and with some easily found clams, wild fruits such as the coconut, and the things which grew of their own accord in the gardens, he had eaten his fill each day. He had suffered from nothing worse than loneliness. He was a heavily built man, slow in his thoughts, and actions. In two years he had grown much fatter, and now had a paunch that hung over the belt of his tattered drawers, and cheeks which shook. While his spirits had sometimes been low, especially at night, he had never given way to despair. He was confident that he would be rescued because he felt certain that he was not castaway on an altogether unvisited island. His hopes of rescue had been much buoyed by finding, early on, a cache containing a pistol, powder, a bag of sea-biscuit, a lantern, and one or two other items suitable for a castaway. It was the custom of Her Majesty's Navy at this time to leave such caches on remote islands, and to call, every so often when their duties permitted, to rescue any unfortunate who might be there. Matthew Bunt was therefore sure that in due course he would be rescued and so it turned out.

One tranquil and brilliant morning, he was dozing under the shade of a palm tree when he was astonished to hear distant voices. Rubbing his eyes, he saw that a frigate had rounded the promontory and cast anchor. A boat, filled with men, was now rowing towards the beach. Matthew Bunt stood up and gazed irresolutely at the spectacle. A man in the bow of the boat, observing him through a spy-glass, waved and hullo'ed. Matthew Bunt did not respond, but stood, his arms to his sides, and his mouth slightly open. The boat beached and Matthew saw men in the uniform of Her Majesty's Navy leap out.

When, a moment later, he saw a man in a heavily laced coat step ashore, he recognized that he must be the captain of the ship, and Bunt's old habits of discipline reasserted themselves. He walked down to the beach and when he was within a suitable distance, drew himself up, and with such dignity as his lack of clothing and his paunch allowed, he saluted.

The master of the frigate, Captain Overton, although normally a stern and gloomy man, greeted this salute with an outstretched hand and a perceptible softening of his usually rigid features. Captain Overton was not surprised to find that tears were pouring down the castaway's cheeks.

'Sergeant Bunt,' said Matthew Bunt, 'of Her Majesty's Marines, in *Orion*,' he said, naming his late ship.

'Stand easy, Sergeant Bunt,' said the Captain, with some emotion. 'I am Captain Overton, Royal Navy, Her Majesty's ship *Achilles*. You may shake hands.'

The two men shook hands, and three more junior officers, following their captain's example, also took Matthew Bunt's hand, the most junior officer of all venturing to place his left hand on the castaway's shoulder.

Matthew Bunt, the tears continuing to roll down his cheeks, said nothing. The officers waited for their captain to speak and Captain Overton sought for words suitable for an officer to address to a sergeant of Marines in such unusual circumstances.

'You will be glad to know, my man,' he said finally, 'that most of your comrades got to safety.'

'Yes, sir,' said Matthew Bunt.

There was a lengthy silence on the sunlit beach, broken only by the gentle lapping of the waves and the calls of a few tropical birds.

'Well,' said Captain Overton, at last, 'since I am ashore and you are the senior rank here – but wait a bit, wait a bit! Are you alone?'

'Yessir.'

'Good. Then you will kindly escort me to some place in the shade where I can hear your report. Ah, yes. Mr Wilkins,' he said, speaking to one of the officers, 'there is a case-bottle in the long boat. Give the Sergeant a tot of rum.'

While this was being done the Captain looked about him and studied the lie of the land. Matthew Bunt took a small mug, drained the rum, and handed the mug back in silence.

'Mr Wilkins,' said the Captain.

'Yes, sir.'

'I think we might have a tot of rum all round. See to it, Mr Wilkins, if you please. I shall meanwhile take a short stroll along the beach to offer up thanks for this deliverance.'

He walked away, his hands behind his back and his hat under his arm. At a distance of some twenty paces, he bowed his head. The officers and sailors meantime silently drank rum. After three minutes, Captain Overton clapped his hat on his head and walked briskly back. The last sailor hastily swallowed his tot and the officers stood once more in attentive attitudes. It was clear that Captain Overton was a respected, and serious, man.

'Now, Sergeant,' said Captain Overton briskly, and Matthew Bunt led him up to the beach where a fallen palm tree lay conveniently in some shade. The Captain seated himself and Matthew Bunt stood to attention. He was no longer weeping, but there were still tear-stains on his ample cheeks.

'Stand easy, Sergeant Bunt,' said the Captain. 'Stand easy, my man. This may be a long business. Tell me first what you remember of what happened when *Orion* struck.'

*

When Bunt had done this to the best of his ability and to the Captain's satisfaction, the Captain said:

'Then you swam ashore?'

'Yes, sir.'

And you found the island deserted?'

'Yes, sir. There had been some natives, sir, but – '

'I know, I know, I know,' said Captain Overton. 'I was here four years ago. They'd already gone. By the way, did you find the cache I left for just such an eventuality as this?'

'Yes, sir. Very handy, it was sir, if I may venture to say so.'

The Captain eyed him.

'Wasn't there a razor in it, Bunt?'

Matthew Bunt reddened. He rubbed his beard nervously.

'Yes, sir.'

'No mirror, perhaps.'

'Not that I can recall, sir.'

'I'll remember next time,' said Captain Overton. He added, with some sarcasm: 'We aim to do our best for the Marines, you know, Sergeant.'

'Yes, sir.'

'Well, never mind. And so you have been on this paradise for two years.'

'About that, sir.'

'Didn't you keep a calendar?'

'No, sir.'

'You should have notched a pole, Bunt.'

'Yes, sir. I'll remember next time, sir,' said Bunt. The Captain glanced up sharply, but never was a man farther from an impertinence than Matthew Bunt. His cheeks were sagging, his lips were dry and there was more sweat on his forehead than was justified by the morning sun.

'Did you never read *Robinson Crusoe*, Bunt?'

'My mother read it to me, sir.'

'Good. Good. A fine book, Bunt. It shows what a man can do with his own two hands to overcome the most adverse fate, provided he is serious minded and energetic. It was for years my favourite book, sergeant. I may tell you that when I think of you here, alone, for two whole years, and of all the opportunities you have had of testing your character and overcoming difficulties, I envy you, Bunt. I have often dreamed of living alone on an island, and only my duties as an officer have prevented me from doing so. Well, now,' said the Captain, getting up, 'show me round your little kingdom, Sergeant Crusoe.' The Captain, saying this, smiled for the first time since he landed. 'First the stockaded hut, and the wheat patch and the goat pen, and so on. This promises to be one of the most interesting days of my life, Bunt. Forward!'

Matthew Bunt hesitated.

'I'm afraid that there are no goats on the island,' he said. 'I'm sure I'm very sorry, sir.'

'Never mind, never mind,' said the Captain. 'Your stockade, then, and your storeroom.'

'My . . . what did you say, sir?'

'The place which you've built to live in,' said Captain Overton, impatiently.

'Oh yes, sir,' said Bunt miserably, and he led the way along the beach, but in a most dejected manner. Nor were his spirits any way improved to see the three officers, at a signal from Captain Overton, fall in behind with expressions as eager as that of their commander.

*

He led them across the beach, over a place where grasses grew among the sand, and then between some coconut palms. Among these, round a clearing, were the grass huts that the islanders had abandoned.

'Here, sir,' he said, desperately, 'is where I live.'

Like the newcomers, he looked around him. Never had the place seemed so ruined. There was not a grass wall without a gaping hole; not a roof that did not sag; and he was surprised that one man with so few possessions could cause such a litter, even if he had not swept up for two years.

'Admirable!' said Captain Overton. 'Most ingenious! I would never have thought of that myself. Would you, Mr Wilkins?'

'No, sir,' said the officer smartly. Then after a suitably respectful pause. 'I'm not sure, sir, that I've even thought of it now.'

'Why, Mr Wilkins, don't you see?' said Captain Overton with great animation. 'Think of Robinson Crusoe. Don't you remember the great pains he took to conceal his dwelling for fear of hostile natives? Sergeant Bunt here solved the problem much more simply and put himself to no trouble at all. He just left this deserted settlement exactly as he found it.' Captain Overton swung his arm in a semicircle; the sun gleamed on the lacing of his cuff. 'Who, looking at this depressing scene of utter neglect, would ever imagine that a human being lived here? A cannibal himself could not be so filthy and untidy in his habits, much less a shipwrecked Englishman. Your home, I take it,' he said, turning to Matthew Bunt, 'lies behind those bushes?'

'No, sir.'

'Then where is it, where, my fine fellow?' said the Captain, with the affable air of one who confesses himself beaten in a game. 'Devil take me if I can see it.'

'Would you be meaning the place where I lived when I first came here, sir?'

'At any time, Bunt, at any time.'

'Well, sir,' said the Marine, pointing. 'I lived in that house for a while.'

It was the worst ruin of all. One wall stood upright, two leaned perilously, and the fourth wall, like the roof, was flat on the ground. 'Then,' said Bunt licking his lips, 'when that fell down one night in the wind, I moved, in a manner of speaking, sir, to the next one. As you can see, sir, the roof of that one got to be none too good and so I upped stakes, sir, as you might say, and moved to the next one, and then . . .' The hopelessness of his position overwhelmed him. He drew a long breath and said, in the voice of a man declaring himself ready for the gallows, 'my present quarters is that there, sir, the last on your left.' He looked at the hut wistfully. Even though he could now see the tear in the roof, the charred wall where it had once caught fire a little, and the mud outside where he threw slops from his cooking basin, it still had, for him, the pull on his heartstrings of home.

Captain Overton said nothing, but the muscles of his tightly clenched jaws were working. He walked to the hut, bent almost double at the low door, and went inside. There was a pause, and then with a gleam of gold braid that was almost dimmed by the flashing of his eyes, he emerged.

'Sergeant Bunt!'

Now that the worst was upon him, Bunt decided to face it like a Marine. He drew himself up to attention. He put his hands stiffly to his side. He held up his chin. He tried to pull in his stomach but found that his muscles had lost the habit.

'Yessir.'

'Where have you put the things you took from the wreck?'

'I didn't take anything from the wreck, sir.'

'I am speaking,' said Captain Overton slowly, 'with particular reference to a box of gold coin, the property of Her Majesty the Queen.'

'Yes, sir. I didn't take nothing, sir.'

'You swam out to the wreck?'

'No, sir.'

'How long was the wreck on the rocks before it sank?'

'Three months, sir.'

'And you never once swam out?'

'No, sir.'

Captain Overton raised his foot and stamped hard on the ground.

'God damn my eyes,' he roared, 'what *were* you doing with your time, then? Answer me!'

'Sitting, sir. And gathering bananas and coconuts: and eating, sir. And sleeping, of course, sir. And . . . and . . .' said Bunt, desperately 'walking, sir; round the island and back again.'

'Nothing else?'

'Nothing much, sir.'

Captain Overton gave him a long and searching look. Then, turning to the senior officer, he said, sharply:

'Mr Wilkins.'

'Sir?'

'You are accustomed to carry along with you a small pocket Bible. Will you be so good as to give it to me?'

'It's a Prayer Book, sir,' said Wilkins, producing a small

leather-bound volume, which the Captain took. Captain Overton turned back to Bunt.

'Take this book in your left hand. As your present commanding officer I instruct you to regard this Prayer Book, containing extracts from the Holy Scriptures, as a Bible. Raise your right hand. Say after me: "I swear to tell the truth, the whole truth, so help me God." ' Matthew Bunt swore. 'Mr Arkwright and Mr Thompson,' continued the Captain, speaking to the two junior officers, 'you are witnesses that Sergeant Bunt has taken a formal oath to tell the truth. Now, Bunt – where – did – you – put – the – things – you – took – from – the – ship?'

'So help me, sir, I didn't . . .' said Bunt, but words failed him. Tears welled once more into his eyes. 'I forgot,' he said in a small, propitiating voice, 'to kiss the book, sir.' He kissed it. He was about to hand it back to Mr Wilkins, when, in an attempt to do something to repair the twenty-four months of contented, squalor in which he had lived, he rubbed the cover of the Prayer Book carefully against his tattered drawers. Mr Wilkins took it from him.

'Mr Wilkins,' said the Captain, 'you will take Mr Arkwright and Mr. Thompson, and you will search the huts.' He then walked deliberately away, and turning his back on Bunt, he clasped his hands under his coat-tails and ostentatiously stared out to sea.

*

Mr Wilkins reported.

'Nothing, sir,' he said.

'Nothing from the ship at all?'

'No, sir. Not a button. It appears he was telling the truth. There's just native bric-à-brac and the things from the cache that I left myself, sir, on your orders.'

There was a silence.

'There *is* just one thing, sir.'

Bunt drew a sharp breath, but did not stir.

'Yes, Mr Wilkins.'

'I hardly like to mention it, but it's a sort of idol, sir. In the second hut from the left.'

'I'm not interested in ju-jubes, Mr Wilkins.'

'No, sir. But this ju-jube is made up, partly, of Admiralty property.'

'Show me it. Bunt, follow us.'

Bunt deliberately played for time.

'Please, Captain, I think if you search the reef outside the lagoon, you'll find plenty of flotsam, sir. It's the reef keeps everything off, sir. I've noticed it.'

'Oh, you have, Bunt. Have you visited the reef?'

'No, sir.'

'And why not?'

'It seemed a long way off, sir. In this climate. I . . .'

'Here it is,' said Mr Wilkins, and he dragged out into the sunlight a large sheet of tarpaulin. Rocking to and fro on it there were two or three bundles of cloth shaped very roughly into the shape of a female body. On top of these was a wooden head, carved with care if no skill, on which was drawn, with charcoal, a face with rose-bud lips. Rope, teazed out, served to represent hair.

Bunt hid his face in his hands.

'Sergeant Bunt,' said the Captain.

'Yes, sir,' said Bunt through his hands.

'What is this . . . this object?'

Bunt raised a ravaged face.

'That, sir,' he said, not without dignity, 'is Lola.'

'That will do, Mr Thompson,' said the Captain, as the youngest officer guffawed. 'So this is Lola, Sergeant. I take it that you spent your time manufacturing this object instead of doing your duty?'

Bunt wiped his face with his hands. He braced his shoulders.

'May I speak, sir?' Captain Overton nodded. 'I'm sure you are right, sir, and I should have been doing my duty. I meant to, but somehow time slipped by and I didn't. If I'd done it, sir, I don't suppose I'd have been lonely. But I *was* lonely, sir. I wanted some company, sir. I wanted it bad.'

'So you made this ... this ...'

'So I made Lola, sir. Yessir.'

'Why did you call her Lola, Bunt. After an acquaintance of yours, perhaps?'

'No, sir. It just came to me, sir, one evening, when she was finished. 'Lola, I said, Lola me girl, you and me –'

'You talked to it?'

'Oh yes, sir. Every evening. We had long conversations, sir. I was very grateful to her, sir, after my wife died.' He said this with such feeling that all four officers looked at him in consternation.

'Was your wife aboard the ship, Sergeant Bunt?' asked Captain Overton. 'I had no idea ...' He broke off, and following the example of his junior officers, he turned to where Bunt, with a gesture eloquent of grief, was pointing. They now saw, for the first time, that behind one of the huts was an oblong plot, with a few blossoming flowers. It was the only tidy place in the vicinity.

'Hats off, gentlemen,' said Captain Overton.

'Yes,' said Matthew Bunt. 'I had to kill her off when Lola came.' Hearing Wilkins's exclamation of horror, he recollected himself. 'Oh, it's not what you gentlemen think,' he said, reassuringly. 'My wife over there's just like Lola. I made her first. I meant to go straight with her, but I dunno. It's the climate, I suppose. I started making Lola, just for a bit of variety, as you might say, and then the fat was in the fire.'

Young Mr Thompson, struggling with himself, felt that he must say something or burst. 'You mean, Bunt,' he said with a preternaturally solemn expression, 'your wife quarrelled with Lola?' He clapped his hand over his mouth and regarded Bunt with large round eyes.

'Yes,' said Bunt, simply.

'I'd be obliged to you, Mr Thompson, if you'd leave this matter to me,' said Captain Overton. 'Sergeant Bunt, am I to understand that in dereliction of your duty as a non-commissioned officer of Her Majesty's Marines, instead of salvaging valuable property from the wreck *Orion*, instead of making yourself a clean, hygienic and defensible bivouac, instead of keeping your body hardy and your hands busy, you lolled and squatted in the sunshine like an ignorant blackamoor, stuffing yourself with bananas and contriving obscene and immoral effigies? Correct me if I am wrong, Sergeant Bunt.'

'It wasn't immoral at first, sir,' said Matthew Bunt. 'I said as how the first one was my wife.'

'Are you married, Bunt?'

'You mean really married, sir?'

'I mean married, you lunatic,' bellowed Captain Overton. 'Is there a Mrs Bunt, God save her perishing soul, back in England?'

'No, sir. I think p'raps, if there had been, I'd have had something to occupy my mind like.'

'But as it is, you could find nothing but . . . but Lola?'

'Yes, sir.'

'You couldn't think by chance about your profession?'

'Profession? Oh, I see what you mean, sir,' said Bunt. 'Well, sir, I've been a marine, man and boy, now for twenty-five years and I can't say that thinking's ever come in my line of duty, begging your pardon, I'm sure.'

'And religion, Bunt. Have you no religion?'

'Oh yes, sir. I was brought up very strict, sir.'

'You were sent to church?'

'Yessir. And Sunday School, sir.'

'And did none of the precepts of your pastors and masters ever cross your mind to lift it even a moment above your . . . your vicious games with your dolls?'

Matthew Bunt bit his lip. He shook his head.

'You would oblige me, Bunt,' said Captain Overton, 'by giving an audible answer when questioned by your superior officer.'

'Yes, sir. On this island, sir, it always seemed Tuesday.'

'Tuesday?'

'Yes, sir. I mean, sir, nobody thinks of religion on Tuesdays, do they sir, not usually.'

'I have known men who think of religion every day of the week, Bunt.'

'Yes, sir. But I wasn't thinking of officers, sir. I was thinking of other ranks.'

Captain Overton drew a long, deep breath.

'Even other ranks,' he said, with a voice which shook with the effort to control himself, 'have been known to address prayers to their Creator on a Tuesday when finding themselves in the dreadful situation of being abandoned on an uninhabited island.'

'Oh *yes*, sir,' said Bunt. 'But I didn't have to worry about that, sir, because I found the cache which you'd so kindly left – I'm sure I'm very grateful, sir, for your forethought – and I knew that –'

Captain Overton interrupted him in a voice that sent the the parakeets fluttering from the branches of the surrounding trees.

'Are you trying to put the blame for your backsliding on ME, you waddling, heap of corruption, you?' asked Captain Overton.

'No, sir,' said Bunt, but no sound came from his bloodless lips.

Captain Overton set about recovering his temper. He had a system for doing this. He did not count ten. Faced with the inadequacies of the world he shut his eyes; he told himself slowly that he was an officer with an unblemished record; and he thanked God that such things could never happen aboard his ship. He then mentally went the rounds, admiring, in his mind's eye, the neatly coiled ropes, the spotless deck, and the shining brasswork, until his spirits were soothed.

Meanwhile, the three officers stood in the sun, furtively dabbing their foreheads, the parakeets returned one by one to their branches, from which they surveyed Captain Overton with outraged eyes, and Bunt wondered if any man had ever been so miserable before.

Captain Overton opened his eyes.

'Come now,' he said, mildly. 'Is there anything else that you have to show me, Sergeant Bunt?'

Bunt clenched his fists. He wetted his dry lips.

'In what way, sir?'

'Well,' said Captain Overton, still under the soothing influence of his brief meditation, 'a little kitchen garden, for instance.'

Bunt sighed windily with immense relief. 'Oh, no. Nothing like that,' he said, with somewhat incautious cheerfulness.

A frown began to gather on the Captain's brow.

'No kitchen garden, eh? Did you grow flowers, perhaps?'

'Oh, no. I just picked them off the bushes.'

'Did you tame any animals?'

'Never saw any animals, sir. It's curious, as I said to myself – '

'Or birds?'

'No, sir.'

'Did you never teach a parrot to talk?'

'I never caught one, sir.'

'Did you,' said Captain Overton, summoning his last recollection of his favourite book, 'build a bower?'

'I beg your pardon, sir. A what, sir?'

'A bower, Bunt. A place in a cool spot where you would take your ease on a sultry night.'

Bunt had a brief struggle with himself, but he knew the outcome of it before it started. He was a middle-aged man. He owed something to what remained of his dignity. He raised his bearded chin a little higher, and looked the Captain in the face.

'I'd rather not answer that question, begging your pardon, Captain Overton.'

'I order you to answer.'

'Yes, sir. But with all due respect, sir, I'd rather not.'

'Are you deliberately flouting my commands, Bunt?'

'I can't do nowise else, sir.'

'Sergeant Bunt, I shall repeat my question slowly, to give you time to reconsider your conduct.'

He repeated it.

Bunt stood silent, his cheeks aflame, but his expression resolute.

'So you persist in your mutinous behaviour?'

'Yes, sir. You can flog me if you like, sir, but I'll not answer your question.'

'Flogging has been abolished in Her Majesty's Navy,' said Captain Overton, 'otherwise I should have been happy to oblige you. However, I can no doubt arrange to have you hanged from the yardarm in Portsmouth harbour with only the slightest delay for a few formalities. Their Lordships at the Admiralty are very sensitive about mutiny, Bunt. Oh, Mr Wilkins.'

'Here, sir,' said Wilkins.

'Get ready to place this man under close arrest.'

Wilkins moved towards Bunt.

'I said "Get ready," Mr Wilkins. I would not like to feel that I had hurried Sergeant Bunt in any way in making up his mind. He has fully ...' He paused and took a large watch from the pocket of his embroidered coat, 'fifteen seconds in which to save his neck,' he said. Captain Overton's virtues shone most brightly when he was a man of action. Now, he stood, relaxed and easy, in perfect control of himself. He watched the face of his watch with no more tenseness than if he had been boiling an egg.

It was quite otherwise with Bunt. The flush drained from his cheeks, only to return more crimson than ever. He wiped his perspiring hands up and down the legs of his drawers. He breathed heavily, and once he groaned.

Captain Overton snapped the cover of his watch into place.

'Well, Bunt?' he said, crisply.

Bunt sagged; his cheeks fell, his head dropped.

'I'll show you, sir,' he whispered. 'Please to follow me.'

*

He led them, barely looking at the path, through clumps of flowering bushes to a place some two hundred yards distant from the village, where there was a low rocky bluff, the first step of the hill which formed the middle of the island. When they had arrived, he pointed silently to a cave, the entrance of which was about eight foot high and four broad.

'There, sir,' he said, and looked fixedly at the ground.

The Captain ran his eyes over the cliff face, the cave entrance, and the ground round about, which was covered with footprints.

'Bunt!'

'Yessir.'

'Look up, man, look up, when I speak to you.'

Bunt raised his eyes with immense reluctance. He carefully avoided looking at the cave.

'What is the meaning of that thing hung on a pole above the opening of that cave?'

'It's a ship's lantern, sir.'

'I can see that for myself. What is it doing there?'

'It's red, sir.'

'I can see that, too. It's the lantern I left so that you could signal if you saw ships' lights in the night. Is that what it is there for?'

'I'm afraid not, sir.'

'Then explain why you put it there.'

'It's a sign, sir,' said Bunt. He passed his hand over his face wearily. 'It's like billiards, in a manner of speaking. It's a sign of a misspent youth. P'raps, if you'd go inside sir, you'll get the information you're seeking.'

Captain Overton was a stern, but he was not a cruel, man. Bunt's misery was so deep and plain that he did as the unhappy sergeant asked him. He went into the cave, he stayed for some minutes, and then he came out. His face was even more set than when he had seen the hut, but there was, in addition, a hint of astonishment in his manner of delivering his next order.

'Mr Wilkins and Mr Arkwright. You will please go into the cavern and take note of what you find there. Do not try to burden your memories with the details. Write them down. No, Mr Thompson,' he said peremptorily, as the most junior officer of all made to follow his companions. Captain Overton barred his way with his gold-braided arm. 'You are too young, Mr Thompson, for this particular duty.'

Captain Overton looked up at the lamp, then at Bunt.

'This cave, I take it, Bunt, was your brothel?'

Bunt swayed.

'Do you mind, Captain, if I sit down?' he said. 'I'm afraid I've come over faint.' With that he sunk down upon a rock, and burying his head in his hands sobbed silently.

'Mr Thompson,' said Captain Overton. 'Go down to the long-boat and bring up the case-bottle. Tell the seamen that they may seek shade if they wish, but they are on no account to move beyond a radius of fifty yards from the long-boat. Return here as quickly as you can.'

Young Mr Thompson cast a longing eye on the cave from which, at that moment, sounded several hearty guffaws.

'Cut along now, Mr Thompson, cut along,' said the Captain, in a surprisingly paternal voice, and Thompson obeyed. As for the guffaws, the Captain for once took no notice at all of such a flagrant breach of decorum. First dusting a rock with his handkerchief, he sat down opposite Bunt.

The two officers inside the cave stood, memorandum books in hand, staring at four neatly laid out female figures, contrived as before, but with a much more brazen hand. The figures sported gay, but exiguous costumes, made out of the set of signal flags which Captain Overton had provided in the cache. On the walls of the cave against which the upper parts of their bodies (composed of gourds and coconut shells) were leaning, Matthew Bunt had drawn charcoal frescoes. These were vivid enough, even although they lacked any sign of what might be called imaginative art. They were, in fact, dimly remembered copies of pictures which Matthew Bunt had seen while on shore leave in various parts of the world, and in various houses of ill-fame.

Their inventory finished, the two officers emerged. They found Thompson had returned and that Bunt was much recovered. He was explaining, with many pauses and broken sentences, how he had come to make the retreat which they had just seen. As far as they could follow, the real cause of it had been Lola, who, after the providential death of Bunt's wife, had been his sole companion on the island. Custom had staled her charms, it seemed, and Bunt had taken to going for long and somewhat ill-tempered walks round the island, especially on moonlit nights. One night, when the moon had been fitfully covered with clouds, he had taken some of Captain Overton's oil and put it in Captain Overton's red lamp to help him light his way. Then, 'just as a joke, sir,' Bunt explained, 'just to get me out of my cross-patch mood with . . . with, well never mind who . . . I hung it up. It's a good lamp, sir, and it burned all night. I slept out, sir, not wanting to go back home, and about three a.m., sir, I woke up and saw it, and well, sir, the idea came into my head like a flash and there you are, sir. It seemed all right at the time, but I do see it was the work of the devil, sir. I do see that now,' he said.

Captain Overton gave no sign. He watched Bunt gravely, as one who did not wish to judge, but who knew what his judgement would be if he did. It was an expression familiar to Bunt from his youth.

Bunt glanced at the two officers with their notebooks in hand.

'You've made a list,' he said guiltily.

'Yes, Bunt.'

'You've put the pink shells down to my credit, I hope, gentlemen. You've at least put them down, haven't you?'

Captain Overton stirred.

'Address your remarks to the senior officer present, Sergeant, which is myself. What shells?'

'Little pink ones, sir. They are very, very hard to find, sir, ones just like that. It might take you hours and it might take you all day, just to find one. Very pretty they are, when you wash them, but very hard to see in the wet sand.'

Captain Overton's stern features softened.

'You collected these pretty shells, Bunt?'

'I did, sir.'

'I am deeply gratified to hear it, Bunt,' said Captain Overton. 'It is my firmest belief that no man is wholly bad. This collecting of shells, Bunt, is the one innocent pastime that you have told us about; the only one, but one is enough. It shall certainly go down to your credit. Gentlemen, see that the shells are properly noted. But why,' he said, with a puzzled frown, 'did you keep them in this reprehensible cavern?'

Bunt, quite carried away by the Captain's praise, said:

'That was the idea, sir. It was a sort of check. I made myself pay one of them every time I went, and since they were difficult to find I – '

'Mr Wilkins,' roared the Captain, jumping to his feet, 'collect every one of those goddammed shells and bring them here at once. I'm going,' he said in a terrible voice, 'to hang 'em round your heathen neck, Bunt, and make you wear 'em from here to Portsmouth gaol.'

But he could not carry out his threat, because there were far too many shells. Mr Wilkins and Mr Arkwright to Mr Thompson's crowing delight, brought them out by hatfuls, and when the last hatful was poured at the Captain's feet, Matthew Bunt tasted the bitter draught of his shame to his last dregs.

*

Recalling it, sitting in the meeting-hall, with the rain beating against the window-panes, Bunt shivered.

Prince put some more coal into the stove.

'Did Captain Overton carry out his threat, Sergeant Bunt?' Prince asked.

'No, sir,' said the Sergeant. 'He kept me in the brig as far as Portsmouth, sir, and then he told me that if I'd learned my lesson, he'd say no more about it than was necessary for the report to Their Lordships and he'd make that brief, "for the sake", he said, "of decency and decorum". Well, that was fine as far as it went, sir, but the officers had their notebooks and well, sir, Portsmouth's a small place, especially when a seafaring man's concerned.' Bunt hung his head for a moment, then sighed, and looked up. 'I asked for my discharge, sir, and came here. I'd got my savings and I bought myself a concession on the beach. Quite profitable it is, too.'

'Which one is it, Sergeant?' asked Prince.

Bunt reddened.

'The ladies' bathing-machine one, sir. And that's it in a nutshell, sir. That's my trouble, sir, that I'd like your advice on. You see, sir,' said Bunt, 'I'm what you might call a religious man. I was brought up strict, sir, and strict I would like to remain. Since I've been on the beach, sir, I'm a regular churchgoer, sir, twice every Sunday and if I can hear an improving sermon in the course of the week, so much the better. I know what's right, sir, and I'd like to do what's right. It's just that I've got this little difficulty over the ladies.

'I know what you re going to say, sir,' he went on. 'You're going to say: "Fight it, Bunt", just as all the other clergymen that I've had the privilege of having a quiet word with. "Fight the devil, Bunt, wrestle with the tempter." Those were the very words of the Vicar of Rottingdean, a nice, kind gentleman, sir, very quiet living. When I spoke to him about the temptations of the flesh, I could see by the way he looked at me that he had *heard* of them all right. Read a book, or something, I daresay. But as for *wrestling*, sir, I don t think he'd done much of it, more's the credit to him, more's the credit.

'But as for me, well, Mr Prince, there's not much about wrestling with temptation I don't know. Half-Nelson, scissors grip, rabbit punching – all in a manner of speaking – I've got the lot at my finger-tips. The devil don't stand a chance with me in fair fight. I wrestle him and I wrestle him and I get his shoulders to the mat and I sit across his chest and I say: "Do you give up or do you want more." And he says: "Sergeant, I give up." So then he gets off the floor, sir, and holds out his hand and says: "Sergeant Bunt, you're a better man than I am." I take his hand, sir, and the next thing I know is that I'm flat on my back.'

'He paused and looked into the fire.

'If you understand me, sir,' he said.

'I do,' said Prince.

'I've sometimes had doubts,' said Matthew Bunt, 'if the Christian faith was quite the one for a religious man like me with my particular obstacles. I've searched around a bit, I must admit. It seems to me that there ought to be a good, sound, respectable church that allows a man who has a weakness for the "ladies" to give way to it – just to save time and bother – without blot-ting his copybook. I can't say that I've found one, as yet.'

Prince put his finger-tips together, he pursed his lips, both for the sacerdotal air it gave him, and for its usefulness in hiding the fact that he was struggling with laughter.

'You might,' he said, 'become a Mohammedan, Mr Bunt.'

'I've thought of that,' said Bunt. 'Being, as you might say, a travelled man, it's come my way, and I know what you mean. But after all, I'm English and proud of it, and it doesn't seem to be – mind you, I'm not saying anything against it – but it doesn't seem to be a very English religion, does it, Mr Prince?'

'So few religions are,' said Prince. 'As you must have noticed in your theological studies, it is singular how many foreigners have managed to push their oar in.'

'They're my sentiments to a T,' said Bunt.

'Are you married, Bunt?' asked Prince.

Bunt looked sadly into the fire for a moment. 'In a manner of speaking, yes, I am.'

Prince, with tact, said nothing.

'It was the first thing I put my mind to when I came back,' Bunt went on, 'especially after the remarks that Captain Overton made on that awful day. But I don't know, Mr Prince, it seems to me there's a lot about this marriage business that nobody's quite thought out.'

'It's not for lack of trying,' said Prince. 'St Paul said –'

' "Better marry than burn," ' quoted Bunt promptly.

'And,' Prince continued, 'theologians have been arguing ever since as to what he meant.'

'It doesn't mean, better marry than fry in hell sir?' said Bunt, deeply interested.

'It might do, Sergeant. On the other hand, it might just mean that it is preferable to marry than be constantly distracted by ... by ...' Prince coughed and sought for words.

'By the ladies,' said Bunt.

'Yes,' said Prince. 'What a useful phrase that is of yours. I must remember it.'

'From my experience,' said Bunt with finality, 'he must have meant hell, sir; because St Paul couldn't be wrong and the other thing doesn't work. I know. I've tried it.'

He undid a button of his coat to ease his paunch a little and continued:

'I wasn't ashore a month, sir, when I found myself a good, honest girl – well, woman she was by that time – that I'd known since I was a boy. She was willing, I was willing, and I'd saved up enough pay to do the thing with an easy mind, so we got spliced – married, that is, begging your pardon for the expression. Now, I've nothing against Nellie. She was a good cook, she kept the house clean, she looked after me hand and foot. But . . .' He stopped.

'She was unfaithful?' suggested Prince.

Bunt shook his ponderous head with a look of great melancholy. 'No, sir. Not Nellie. I was the only man that she ever had eyes for.'

'Very proper, Sergeant.'

'If you'll excuse me,' said Bunt, 'that's just what it wasn't. It was the other way about. A loving wife, a really loving wife, can be a great stumbling-stone to a man what's trying to rise to higher things. No sooner had I settled down by the fire of an evening and composed my thoughts, just as we're sitting here, me with a good book and her with her sewing, than I'd know what she was thinking of.'

'What?' asked Prince, and then, hastily. 'Oh, yes, I see. But that's a wife's privilege, Sergeant, you can't hold it against her.'

'I don't hold it against her personally, Mr Prince. Not against Nellikins. It's the whole idea of the thing that I'm against. I mean, sir, if you'll allow me to mention the topic, a man that's fighting the urge to go out and get himself drunk each evening, for instance, sir, isn't going to be helped if someone sits on the other side of the fireplace hour after hour making a noise like popping corks. Is he, sir? I ask you fairly?'

'And as fairly, Sergeant, I reply, no, he isn't. I confess I had never thought of it like that.'

'Well, if it surprises a learned gentleman like you,' said Bunt, 'you can guess how it puzzled Nellie. "But you love me, Matt," she'd say, with her forehead all wrinkled up and tears not far away, "you love me, Matt, and you're my husband. Don't you want to make me happy?" "Yes, I do, Nellie," I'd tell her and it was no less than the truth, as always with me in dealing with the fair sex. "Well, then, Matt," she would say, "don't be a silly old bear." So I'd make her happy, and in no time at all I was making several other ladies of the town happy, and, of course, Nell found out. She went home to her mother and there she is, poor girl, at this moment. So you see what I mean when I say that not enough thinking has been done about the matter, Mr Prince. It doesn't touch my problem.'

'I don't believe that much thinking has been done recently,' said Prince. 'But a considerable time back, some sixteen hundred years ago, there was quite a deal of discussion about the very problem which is bothering you, Sergeant. That is the ... er ... corks, as you put it. A great number of very holy men, many of whom subsequently became saints, decided that the only way of avoiding temptation was to go off into the wilderness and live absolutely alone –'

'I've done that,' said Bunt, with simplicity. Prince paused. He looked at Bunt.

'By George,' he said, 'so you have. You know, Bunt, you're quite right. Morally, you pose a deeply interesting problem.'

'I'm very glad and honoured to hear you say that, sir,' he said. 'All the time I've been coming to your meetings, I've been saying to myself: "There's the gentleman who can help me, if anybody can." You see, sir, I know you're a very learned clergyman, and besides that, as everybody says, you're partial to the ladies yourself and ...' He stopped. He placed his hand over his mouth. He blushed furiously. He took his hand away from his mouth and said, contritely:

'Cor love me, I shouldn't have said that.'

Prince looked at him for a moment, and then ran his eyes round the empty rows of seats. He sighed deeply.

'Why shouldn't you alone say it? Everybody else does. Yes, Bunt – you were saying that you thought I could help you.'

'If I may presume, sir,' said Bunt, humbly. 'Yes.'

Prince got up and walked a few paces up and down. At the end of one of his promenades he looked over his shoulder at Bunt and asked suddenly:

'*Everybody* is saying it, Bunt, did you say?'

'I beg your pardon, Mr Prince.'

'About myself and the ladies. You may speak quite frankly, Sergeant.'

'It's quite well known – I mean,' said Bunt, correcting himself, 'there's a lot of gossip, all false, of course, as it always is.'

'Not always, Bunt,' said Prince. 'Not always.' He took hold of the lapels of his coat and resumed his walk, looking intently at the bare floor boards. Bunt watched in a respectful silence.

Prince came up to the fire. Still holding his lapels he looked down at the heavy figure of Bunt, and smiled. It was, as his female disciples said, a very beautiful smile.

'Sergeant Bunt,' he said, 'clergymen have their secrets just as other people do.'

'I'm sure I'm very sorry if I said anything that was impertinent,' said Bunt.

'No, no. Those are not the secrets that I mean,' said Prince, reassuringly. 'I mean we have our little professional secrets. Among them, friend,' he went on, his voice gathering its customary public richness, 'are sermons. The sermons that we preach in the pulpit are very edifying and not at all surprising. But we have little sermons which we preach among ourselves, especially to the younger members of our profession. They are also edifying, but perhaps a little more unexpected. One, I remember, was preached to me by a very wise old bishop, to whom I had gone one day in great anguish of mind. I was struggling, friend, struggling,' he stopped. He smiled broadly and, dropping his rich tones for the briefest instant, said: 'Well, Bunt, it was about the ladies. The bishop, I suppose,' he resumed, once more in his organ tones, 'had preached it to hundreds of young ordinands, and some other bishop had preached it to him. I didn't think a great deal of it at the time; in fact I quarrelled with the bishop who told it me, but as the years have rolled I have had increasing cause to remember it. I am going to tell it you, Sergeant, although it is not the thing that one would ordinarily tell a layman. But I feel, friend, that your faithful attendance at my gatherings has given you some sort of ecclesiastical status, comparable perhaps,' and his eyes twinkled at Bunt who was following him open-mouthed, 'to those dignitaries in the early church as doorkeepers, or ... or yes, exorcists. I am sure, Bunt, you may be regarded as an exorcist, and thus on the lowest rung of the hierarchy, but still, on it.'

'I'm sure I'm very much obliged to you,' said Bunt in an awed whisper.

'Well, friend and fellow cleric,' went on Prince, 'I had poured out my difficulties to his Lordship, and his Lordship replied that I must not agitate myself so. They were sore trials, very sore trials, but we must not try to delve too deeply into the intentions of Providence. All was for the best, his Lordship was sure, although it was all very puzzling. Yes, indeed, even my Lord the Bishop confessed he was puzzled. For instance, there was the instance of Frederick and of George that his Lordship had come across. Frederick and George were brothers, their births being separated by but a single year. Frederick grew up to be a very careless fellow, a gay dog, who took to the primrose path so naturally that, as one might say, he even lingered to pick himself posies of that seductive flower. Many bright eyes shed tears because of Frederick, many a maiden's heart was broken – you understand, Bunt, that I am not using phrases that I would personally prefer. I am quoting a bishop – many sweet girls had their innocence for ever darkened by the impulsive Frederick.

'But George was different. He was no less hot-blooded than Frederick. Were they not brothers? But he was made of finer clay. He wrestled with temptation, mightily, and he fought long and hard. Sometimes, sometimes, he fell. We are all sons of Eve, and cannot hope to be perfect. But when he fell, he quickly rose again, although his remorse was terrible. He grew wan and pale, fighting that good fight, while Frederick, who had forgotten even that he ought to fight, grew rosy and fat.'

'It's a strange world,' whispered Bunt. 'Go on, sir.'

'For all that, both George and Frederick lived to a goodly age. They both reached eighty, and passed it. George was a frail old gentleman. Frederick was as fresh complexioned as a baby. So much for their bodies. As for their souls, George, at last, after all his trials, had triumphed. He was free, finally, from the desires of the flesh.' Prince bent his head. He looked up. 'And so was Frederick,' he finished, smiling on his listener benignly.

'Just fancy,' said Bunt in hushed voice, 'just fancy a bishop talking as much sense as that.'

'Just fancy,' said Prince.

Then the door opened and Julia came in, carrying a large tray with several steaming dishes on it, followed by the caretaker with yet another.

'Look,' she said, holding the door back with her foot. 'Look at all the lovely things Mrs Cusack's been getting ready. Oh,' she observed that Prince was still grasping the lapels of his coat. 'Oh, I'm so sorry. Were you preaching?'

'Yes,' said Matthew Bunt, reverently. 'He was preaching wonderful.'

Prince took his hands away, and said:

'I have just preached the finest sermon in my life, Julia, my dear, but it is quite finished.' He took the tray from her and kissed her on the forehead.

'Now,' he said, 'let us eat. Mr Matthew Bunt, my dear, is a man of great moral perspicacity. Ask him to join us.'

On the tray that Mrs Cusack carried were glasses and a jug of punch; on the tray that Prince held were plates of cakes, a plate of toast, half a pigeon pie, knives, forks, and a letter.

'Oh!' said Prince, with a groan. 'A letter.'

'Yes,' said Julia. 'It came this morning, but I forgot to give it to you. I didn't think you were much in a mood for letters in any case.'

Prince nodded.

He now took the letter and one of the knives. He slit it open, sighing as he did so.

'Among the many virtues of the ladies on your island, Bunt,' he said, 'is that they had never learned to write. One of the trials

42

of a clergyman's life that they omitted to warn us about at the theological college was these·– ' He waved a bulky letter in the air. 'Holy missives from women of all ages. I suppose they left it to our intelligence. After all, the very earliest Christians,' he said, as he began to read, 'were indefatigable letter writers . . . Good God!' he said suddenly.

'It's not that woman after a lock of your hair, is it?' said Julia, and as Bunt helped her pull a table to the stove, she explained to him: 'A really dreadful woman, Mr Bunt. It is not so much that she wants a lock of Mr Prince's hair. I don't mind that. But she will keep referring to it as a "relic".'

'Very grisly, ma'am,' said Bunt. Prince continued to read his letter while the table was set, and even while he ate his pie. At last he said:

'Julia, do you remember the Five Signs?'

'Yes, Henry.'

Mrs Cusack, who was moving round the table seeing that her guests had plenty to eat, snorted, as she always did when any of Prince's female admirers were mentioned.

'They were five sisters,' he said to Bunt. 'You may have seen them sometimes when you came to meetings. Mrs Prince and I called them The Five Signs from Heaven, because they were all unmarried, and their father was rich.'

'Yes, I do remember them,' said Bunt, munching his pie. 'I remember seeing the old gentleman slip a sovereign into the collecting bag. And if you'll pardon the impertinence, sir, wouldn't a plate be better? It steps up the collection, if I may say so. It's what we always found when we had a whip-round aboard ship.'

'That,' said Prince, 'is yet another thing they failed to teach us at the theological college. In fact, I cannot recall what they did teach us, except religion, and that only with the greatest reluctance. Well, this time, the old gentleman's put one hundred pounds in the bag.' He waved a banker's draft. 'And he wants me to go to London to give him advice about his daughters. He's had a stroke, I gather. Well,' he said to Julia, 'what do you think of that?'

'A hundred whole pounds!' said Julia. 'Henry, promise me here and now that at least thirty pounds of that money goes on buying yourself some new clothes.'

'I promise, Julia,' said Henry: and, to Bunt, 'If this little glimpse of the private life of the English clergy does not overcome your scruples about becoming a Mohammedan, then nothing will.'

'Henry,' said Julia. 'Henry, when you talk to him, do remember he's not a bishop, won't you. Don't bite his head off.'

'I shall be as smooth as balm in Gilead,' said Prince. 'Since he is rich enough to throw away a hundred pounds and he has been quite unable to marry off five daughters, I shall suggest that he uses his wealth to build them a nunnery. Or ...' said Prince, 'or ...' He slowly laid down his knife and fork.

'Or what, Henry?' asked Julia.

He looked at his wife with a curious expression.

'Or nothing, my dear,' he said. 'What a very good pigeon pie this is.'

'Five unmarried daughters and plenty of money,' said Bunt, musingly. 'They were quite pretty, one or two of them. At any rate, they weren't battleaxes, if you'll overlook the expression, Mrs Prince. It certainly looks as if there's a bit of a mystery.'

Bunt was correct; there was a mystery, and since the mystery played a large part in the founding of the Abode of Love, we must now turn our attention to the Five Signs, and their father, Josiah Nottidge.

3

The Random Wooings

JOSIAH NOTTIDGE, their father, was a timber merchant. He was not very interested in timber but he sold his wood with ease and profit for some twenty years and at the end of that time he had found himself a rich man. Thousands of merchants had done the same thing but Josiah was not like any of them. He did not wax fat; he did not grow pompous; he did not yearn to be received into society. He merely remained what he had always been, a rather short, rather thin, very bored timber merchant, who drummed with his fingers on the arm of his chair and sometimes hummed to himself. That is, he was like this until he began to be as fascinated by the mysteries of money, as Prince had become fascinated by the mysteries of religion, which was in his fifty-second year. Then he changed. He became lively, rubicund, and garrulous. He had suddenly found that one large part of living – all that part which had to do with money – was the most delectable nonsense.

His only trouble was that he could find no one to talk to about his discoveries. All his friends were in the timber trade, and they took money very seriously. As for his five daughters, he was very fond of them, but he had to admit that they were of no help in the matter. They understood money so little that they could barely add up their change when they went shopping: consequently they took money even more seriously than the timber merchants, and when their father tried to draw them into conversation on the topic, they would burst into tears and send their new hats back to the milliners. But Josiah was not concerned with their saving money – or with their spending it. He wanted them to think about it, to study it in all its beautiful, lunatic ways and above all – for this was his real hobby – to relish the extraordinary effects that money had on human beings.

To understand Josiah's late passion, we should understand how he had spent the earlier part of his life. He had imported exotic wood and sold it. This was such a simple thing to do that Josiah often wondered if there could possibly be as simple a way of earning a living. After some thought and much drumming on the arm of his chair he had decided that he could think of only one, and that was holding horses. It struck him as curious that people who held horses made very little money while he was worth a hundred thousand pounds: but beyond that, money had at first made no impression on him. It came too easily. The people who sold him teak, or mahogany, or smooth black logs from ebony trees, had to bargain with the owners of manacled slaves, or with mahouts, waving goads red with the blood from elephants' ears, or with fat, sly Brahmins who had two boys to lean on when they wheezily came to bargain. They paid in rupees, cowrie, and Maria Theresa dollars. They died of strange diseases or solaced themselves with even stranger love. Josiah Nottidge sat from nine till seven in a counting-house in Bermondsey, saw his unvarying customers, yawned, and stirred the fire, and grew rich.

Then one day his wife died, and her brother took the occasion of the funeral to ask Josiah to lend him some cash. The brother-in-law named the sum, which was a large one, but when Josiah asked him what it was for, he said he must respect Josiah's grief and tell him at the counting-house. This he did, some weeks later. He was an eager, nervous man, full of new ideas and the spirit of the age. He wanted to open a furniture shop. This was very novel because people at that time built up their furniture piece by piece over the generations and if they wanted a new piece they went to a carpenter, who built it with so much care for its lasting that he might have been making a coffin for a Pharaoh. Josiah's brother-in-law, however, said that modern, up-and-coming Victorians were in too much of a hurry for these ponderous ways. They made money quickly and they wanted everybody to know it with the same celerity. Josiah's brother-in-law planned to open a shop where they could furnish a house in an afternoon. Josiah lent him the money for the sake of his

46

dead wife, and for ten per cent per annum. He was not particularly impressed by the chances of the shop's success, but he
said he'd give it three years and then take a second look at the
whole thing. The brother-in-law wrung Josiah's hand gratefully
and, quivering with enterprise, rushed from the counting-
house.

The shop was opened and the customers began to come, first
in a trickle, then a stream. When they came in a flood somebody bought a building on the other side of the road and opened
another furniture shop selling exactly the same furniture.
Josiah's brother-in-law took this very hard.

He was, as we have seen, filled with the spirit of the times, but
he had not learned that the essence of success is that it is never
necessary to think of a new idea oneself. It is far better to wait
until somebody else does it, and then to copy him in every
detail, except his mistakes.

To meet this competition, Josiah's brother-in-law worked
night and day. He designed furniture of a weight and splendour
that had not been seen since the days of Louis XIV. It was
admired, bought, and a month later faithful replicas appeared in
the rival shop window. Both shops flourished, but since Josiah's
brother-in-law was doing all the thinking, he grew thin with
worry, while his rival grew sleek. Customers fell into the habit
of visiting both shops before they made a purchase. When they
left the shop of Josiah's brother-in-law for the one across the
road, they hurt both his pocket and his pride; when they
crossed the street in the opposite direction they only hurt the
owner's pocket. What with his long hours, his injured pride and
his nervous constitution, Josiah's brother-in-law began to grow
sickly and at last downright ill in bed.

One day, Josiah was stirring his fire as usual and beginning to
yawn when he suddenly closed his mouth. An idea had come to
him. He stared at the fire for a few minutes, then laid the poker
carefully down on the fender, took his hat off its peg and went
out.

First he visited the rival shop across the road and spoke for a
while to its owner. Then he came out of the shop, accompanied

by its bobbing and bowing proprietor, was handed into a cab and was driven to the house of his brother-in-law. A distraught wife showed him up to his brother-in-law's bedroom, where he found the shopkeeper lying prostrate in bed, with his face a vivid yellow from an attack of jaundice. When he saw Josiah his eyes rolled in their hollows and he burst into tears. He sobbed that the business was going to ruin, he bewailed the doctor's bills that he was running up, and he chokingly confessed that he would probably have to fall short a little in paying Josiah his interest. At this awful news his wife, a good woman, also burst into tears, freely prophesying that the whole family would end up in the debtors' gaol.

When the noise had diminished, Josiah consoled them. First he told them that for the entire period in which his brother-in-law lay ill, he would ask for not one penny of interest on his money. Next, he told him that he would give him six months' credit for the raw wood, which by agreement had to be bought exclusively from Josiah. Lastly, he turned to the wife and told her that the doctor's bill should be sent to him, Josiah, and he would pay it. All that he wanted to see, he added, was his brother-in-law well again and fit to give that thieving, rival shop the trouncing it deserved.

On the receipt of these three pieces of news, Josiah's brother-in-law dragged himself into a sitting posture in order to kiss his benefactor's hand, his wife flung herself on Josiah's bosom and was removed only with difficulty, and when Josiah did at last manage to get downstairs to the cab, she stood in the rain, calling blessings down on Josiah's head, while a yellow face could be seen pressed against the bedroom window-pane and a yellow hand feebly waved in a farewell salute.

In the cab Josiah Nottidge took out a handkerchief, dabbed his eyes, blew his nose and then marvelled all the way back to his office. He had good cause, for he had just made arrangements to ruin the family which was calling down blessings upon his ingenious head. He had bought his way into the rival shop, on the understanding that with the new money its proprietor would beat the daylights out of his brother-in-law's shop, if he could. The proprietor had sworn that he would stop at nothing this side of the law to put the other shop out of business. Since he was down to his last ten guineas, he was willing and eager to agree to buy all the wood that would be expended in this war exclusively from Josiah Nottidge.

When Josiah got back to his counting-house he reflected that he had done a despicable act, and its victims had asked God to bless him. The more he pondered on this, the more astonished he was at what money could do. He had at last found an interest in life.

The doctor's bill turned out to be a small one because Josiah's brother-in-law, his blood warmed and his bowels stirred by Josiah's kindness, quickly got better. He set to work so hard that the man across the road had to double his staff to keep pace in his copying. Both shops were crowded all day with customers; both kerbstones were lined with spanking new carriages; both shops made Josiah bounding profits from the wood they used, and added to his delight by paying him his interest with great regularity. The rival proprietors never met, although they were always present in each other's thoughts; and both proprietors continued to call Josiah Nottidge a thundering fine fellow.

Josiah Nottidge began to feel that he must be: his conscience told him that he was a knave and a double dealer – every month more so because he gained more and more money and grew richer and richer on other men's labours. But, on the other hand, he observed with growing fascination that if he stopped being a knave and took his money back into his timber business where it had been before, he would be called a skinflint, a turn-coat, a miser and a snatcher of bread from little children's mouths. So he marvelled, and prospered, and in due course became an alderman.

Now the five daughters of Josiah Nottidge, timber merchant of Bermondsey, had never any serious suitors. But the five daughters of Josiah Nottidge, Alderman, were agreeably surprised to find that they had considerable attraction for the opposite sex. Previously, when they had gone to the rare ball which came their way, they had been forced to sit self-consciously in a row for hour upon hour, like a portion of a frieze portraying the more serious Muses. This had become so embarrassing that they had developed little techniques to give animation to the tableau. Harriet, the eldest, would feel faint, and have to be taken into the open air; Agnes would lose her fan and it would have to be searched for; while Clara, Cornelia and young Louisa, if there was positively nothing else they could do, would go, one by one, to the bathroom.

Now, however, none of these devices was necessary. The younger sons of other aldermen, propelled in the direction of the sisters by beaming fathers, would bow and ask them to dance. They were generally rather serious young men, who, when they fetched the sisters jellies, were inclined to talk of mahogany. But the Nottidge sisters did not mind: they were prepared to talk of old tin trays as long as they were answered in a male voice.

But then, at last, came a young man, who talked of battles, and charges, cannonades and booty; a young man who wore a dashing uniform and who smelt deliciously when you leaned close, of tobacco. He was an ensign who had seen brief service in the Coromandel, and who had been sent home because he lost too heavily at cards. He had no money but he had a fine moustache, and his first name, romantically, was Eustace. He danced with the sisters and sat with them in the intervals. Harriet never felt the need for air, Agenes's fan was as though glued to her fingers, and Clara, Cornelia and Louisa had no more need to go to the bathroom than archangels. They met him at a ball, at a rout, at a reception and lastly in their own home. They were breathless and sleepless, waiting to see which of them was the attraction. Then, one day, they all went walking in Richmond park, played a demure form of tag among the trees. That evening, Clara, combing out her hair in front of the mirror said, 'Eustace kissed me.'

Four hearts stood still. Then Clara turned from the mirror and looked at them. Four sisters saw the family face of which they had learned to despair, but it was changed. She was no longer plain. In fact, she never had been; the Nottidge sisters although they were spinsters were none of them unhandsome, and as Sergeant Bunt had noticed, Clara, Agnes and young Louisa were pretty. But they had seen one another's faces daily for many years, and it was as though they had spent those years constantly in front of an unflattering mirror. The family forehead was broad; they thought it bony. The family nose was thin; they thought it too long; the family eyes, they had to admit, were lively, and their lips were well-formed; but only Louisa and Agnes had the correct demure expression; the others, in unguarded moments, were inclined to look brassy, or so they thought. Now Clara turned, from the mirror, and looked at them, and they saw, for the first time, that she was beautiful. The four sisters, who had thought so much about love, had never thought of this. One by one, they came up to Clara and embraced her, awesomely, as though they embraced a sister returning from a visit to Paradise.

*

When the unlucky four woke up next morning they were inclined to feel rather more critical of their sister; she for her part went about her morning duties with an even richer glow than she had displayed the night before. Agnes, Cornelia and Louisa, reflecting that they would have to live with this irritating refulgence in their midst for a considerable time, lost their tempers and were rude to Clara. But Harriet, the eldest sister, had passed her thirty-fifth birthday, and a spinster of that age has learned how to deal with her emotions. She buttonholed her father as he was leaving for the counting-house, gave him some indication of the lie of the land, and came back with permission to hold such routs, supper parties, theatre-goings and picnics as she thought fit for the occasion. The old gentleman went off whistling, and Harriet flung the household into such a bustle of organization that the three other sisters so far forgot their chagrin as to agree to buy new frocks, all expensive, but all very quiet in taste, so that Clara could shine as the brightest star in their neglected constellation.

Then Harriet set about the business of arranging that the

lovers should be alone. The conventions of the time demanded that they should always be surrounded by every appearance of intense and gregarious social life. Thus, having driven Nature out with a pitchfork, she was allowed to crawl back by a series of well-worn stratagems which resulted in the lovers being left by themselves for carefully measured periods. These intervals of privacy were long enough to inflame desire, but too short for any passion to be slaked, unless it was so violent as to verge on the acrobatic.

Usually, this arrangement was simple enough. Young brothers could be sent off to play, fathers persuaded to read the newspaper in their studies, and a sister sent up to do some sewing. With four sisters, however, the thing needed parade-ground timing; but in Harriet they found an excellent sergeant-major. A dinner party, a theatre party, a reading party and a social evening all had ingenious tactical evolutions, and the lovers were long enough alone for Eustace, one day, to go down on his knee and tell Clara that he wished to marry her. She looked at him lovingly and said that he would have to ask father.

For this tremendous occasion, all five sisters stayed in the drawing-room, while Eustace, shaking with a fright he had never felt when facing the howling Hindoo, tapped at Josiah's study door. He was benignly invited to come in. The drawing-room door was left open, but no raised voices were heard. After half an hour there came the sound of tinkling glasses, and a little later, Josiah, rubicund, chuckling and patting the young man on his shoulder, came into the drawing-room and gave Clara a fatherly embrace. The whole occasion, in a word, went off entirely correctly, except for one thing: Eustace looked profoundly worried.

In the course of the next few days, Eustace's anxiety deepened to such a point that one day when they had been left alone, Clara asked him if her father had disappointed him concerning the dowry. Eustace hastily answered that he had been, on the contrary, quite generous. With the sum that he proposed to settle on Clara and Eustace's army pay, they would be able to live without worry. 'We won't be rich,' said Eustace. 'No, my dear Clara, we shall not be rich by any means. But then, again, my dear, we shall be by no means poor.' With that he kissed her, absently.

Harriet's programme of diversions went its way. Since the fish had been landed, they once more came out in their most splendid clothes; and since Eustace was soon to be a member of the family, they already treated him with something of the freedom they would use towards a brother. All went well until the night they came home, rather tired, from a picnic. This had not been a great success as had been expected. Eustace had, for weeks, been showing a very marked sense of his social duties, although still in a worried manner. He had not neglected any of the sisters; he had parcelled out his time between all five of them in a way which Clara, although admitting it was gentlemanly, thought decidedly irritating. During their last picnic he had refused to be left alone with Clara at all. He had spent a long time out of observation, with Harriet.

The sisters slept in two rooms on the third floor of the house, that were joined by folding doors, so that all could use the commodious dressing-table. Harriet was brushing her hair at the mirror. Clara, getting into her nightgown was questioning Harriet sharply about the incident, as was her right, when Harriet put down the brush, turned and facing them all said:

'Well, if you want to know, Eustace kissed me.'

*

The five sisters stood perfectly still: the five sisters stood perfectly silent. Then Clara said:

'Oh! oh! Then it was *you* who was stealing him away from me. Harriet, you *viper!* I am going to tear your hair out by handfuls.'

If Clara's metaphor carried little conviction, the tone of voice in which she made her threat carried a great deal. As she advanced upon her eldest sister, Harriet rose and said:

'I said that Eustace kissed me. I did not say that I kissed him back. However, I do not expect you to believe me.' She then prepared to defend herself with her hair-brush.

At this moment Cornelia said, in the clear, level, and penetrating voice which was then thought proper for a gentlewoman when quarrelling:

'For that matter, since we are all telling secrets, Eustace kissed me too. And I did kiss him back.'

This flanking attack put Clara – as it is said to put armies – in confusion.

'My Eustace,' said Clara her lips trembling, 'kissed *you*?'

'Yes,' said Cornelia, 'so if you're going to tear Harriet's hair out, you had better tear mine out too. If you can,' she added, folding her arms across her nightgown.

Louisa, the youngest sister, was sitting on the bed, cutting her toe-nails. She looked up from her task for a moment to say:

'I can't think what you'll do with all the hair you're going to collect, Clara dear, but it'll be enough to open a wig-shop, because I saw Eustace kissing Agnes last Tuesday and last *Thursday*,' she said, resuming her cutting, 'he kissed me.'

Clara looked round slowly and wonderingly at her sisters.

'Yes,' said Harriet, sympathetically, 'that makes the lot. I rather feared it. And,' she said, with a sigh, 'I also fear that I was the last on the list. Well, well,' she said, bracing herself with all her thirty-five years, 'it seems that your Eustace is a lady-killer,' and that's that.'

The name was not accurate; four of the Nottidge sisters had never looked more alive. But it unlocked Clara's sorrow, and she burst noisily into tears.

One by one the sisters tried to take her in their arms. One by one they were recognized as vipers by the sobbing Clara; one by one they were spurned with hard words, pushes and for little Louisa, even a well-aimed kick. The noise on the usually quiet third floor grew.

There was disunion even among the vipers. Agnes called Louisa a tell-tale, a spy and a liar. Since Louisa was not a liar, at all, she ripped the ribbon off her sister's nightgown, for which Agnes shook her till she screamed. Harriet, as the eldest, and the only one armed, began to hit Agnes's posterior with the hair-brush to make her let go of Louisa. Cornelia, maintaining the clear and penetrating voice of a gentlewoman but shouting, per-force, above the din, called Harriet a bully, a tyrant, a stuck-up beast and a woman who thought because she was the eldest nobody else in the family had any rights. This had nothing to do with Eustace but it was something that Cornelia was accustomed to say in every family crisis. Its irrelevancy to any matter in hand usually goaded the practical Harriet to fury, but in this unprecedented brawl, it went unnoticed by all, except Josiah Nottidge. He, in nightgown, nightcap and holding a candlestick, stood in the doorway observing the scene. He said, mildly:

'Cornelia, I do wish you could see more merit in your sister, Harriet. She is really a very competent housekeeper, and I am sure we should all be grateful for that.'

He did not, however, press the point, but tranquilly resumed his observation of the scene in front of him.

Harriet bore out her father's good opinion of her, for with her hairbrush, a slap or two, and some sharp commands, she soon restored order, and nothing was left to witness the disturbance save tear-stained cheeks, torn nightgowns, and Clara, still sobbing into her pillow, but quietly.

Josiah Nottidge now came forward and asked if there had been any trouble.

Patting her hair into order, Harriet, blushing to find her father in the room, said:

'I am very sorry, father. We must have woken you up. We are *all* very sorry, are we not?'

The other sisters, who had instantly scrambled into their beds, murmured: 'Yes, Harriet.'

'But we are all rather upset and not quite ourselves, father,' Harriet went on. 'Eustace has been behaving most outrageously.'

'Oh yes?' said Josiah. Then elaborately raising his eyebrows, lowering the candle and bending down, he said: 'And where is he? Under the bed?'

'No, father,' said Harriet. 'He is not under the bed. He is not even in the house and I hope he never will be again. He has been unfaithful to poor Clara.'

'Ah,' said Josiah, straightening up. 'I understand. I understand very well. He has been playing kiss-in-the-ring with all my pretty daughters.'

'Yes, father.'

'Including you, Harriet, my dear?'

'Yes, father.'

'I'm glad of that,' said Josiah, a little mysteriously. 'Well my children, I am afraid Eustace is a very flighty fellow. He has been making proper fools of all of us. I cannot,' he said, with a broad smile, 'say I am altogether surprised. Now, my dears, I shall kiss you all good night and we can all get a night's sleep and excommunicate the dreadful fellow with bell, book and candle in the morning.'

So he kissed them, and went away. The sisters blew out their candles, but they talked until they were too sleepy to talk any more.

'We must get rid of him,' said Clara at last, 'because I'm sure, if we don't we shall have everybody laughing at us.' She yawned. 'Good night, Harriet. God bless.' Three other sisters murmured sleepily 'Good nights'.

'God bless you all,' called Harriet. 'Good night.' And then, as she thumped her pillow, she said, into the darkness. 'It would be quite natural for everybody to laugh at us. Heaven knows, they always do. But why was father so amused. That was very strange indeed.' She thought for a while, but then she, too, felt her eyes close. Soon there was nothing to be heard on the third floor but the regular breathing of the four sisters, and poor Clara, muttering her lost lover's sibilant name in her sleep.

*

Perhaps Eustace would have been reprieved; a woman notoriously has a soft spot in her heart for a libertine and in the Nottidge house there was not one, but five such spots. But

Eustace himself rushed upon his doom. When Clara taxed him with unfaithfulness, he neither denied it, nor was he sorry. Nor for that matter, was he gay or dashing. When Clara fled the room, in tears, Harriet had a word with him. She had no better luck. 'He was glum,' she reported that night, 'but every inch a soldier. I think that is how officers must look at a court-martial. I find it very puzzling; very puzzling indeed.'

Clara had one more try, over tea and cake; she did her best to treat the matter lightly. In a bantering manner she asked him to promise never to flirt with her other sisters again. 'Promise,' she said, with her sugar tongs poised above the cup, 'never to be a naughty boy again.' To which he replied with a most serious expression: 'Miss Clara, I may have been naughty, but I am not a boy. I am an officer and a gentleman and it grieves me to say I cannot candidly promise what you ask.' Clara bit her lip and dropped a lump of sugar into her cup with the expression of one who would prefer to be dropping her lover in the river. The next day Eustace was shown the door in a stiff little note from Harriet, and Josiah, sympathetically, took his five daughters for a holiday to Brighton.

Josiah urged his daughters to amuse themselves, which they did, in their own way. The theatre, the assembly-hall, and their friends' receptions they found insipid. They were much more diverted by religious meetings, particularly those that dealt with the scientific proof from the Bible that the world was about to end. These suited their mood admirably and they became quite jolly. It was in this way that they first came across Henry Prince. They attended one of his meetings. They approved of his theology and even more of his looks. They waited behind once or twice, after the rest of the congregation had gone, in order to have a more personal word with him. In this they were not very successful. Prince willingly spoke to them: but five listening women unavoidably gave the impression of a public meeting, and Prince, still young and enthusiastic (for it was at the outset of his meetings), could not resist the temptation to preach a sermon. But the sisters were satisfied. If they still heard only religion, it was at a much closer range. They agreed among themselves that Prince looked holy, surprisingly young for a man of such wisdom, and that he wanted someone to look after him in a motherly way, or else he would harm his health. They took their father along to a meeting; he scoffed, as they expected. But they noticed that he gave Prince many long and speculative looks. When Josiah told them one day he had a great surprise for them, they thought, with holy joy, that he had saved his soul. Their joy, if less holy, was perhaps even greater when he told them that he had arranged for a talented young artist to paint their portraits. The thought of sitting in front of a young man who would, perforce, look at their faces rather than their immortal spirits, warmed them considerably. They eagerly packed their trunks and set off for London, where the painting was to take place.

The young man, it turned out, was the youngest son of a titled family that had fallen on hard times. He was too poor to own, as yet, a studio, so he set up his easel in the Nottidge conservatory. He had dark, curling hair, an aristocratic nose set between limpid eyes, and he had the most beautiful hands that they had ever seen. He grouped the five sisters together with the utmost artistry, flung drapes here and there with romantic abandon, and when he faced his canvas, he suffered artistic agonies without, they observed, the least touch of ill-breeding. He had not put in three strokes with his charcoal before the sisters unanimously recognized his powerful genius: he had barely done the blocking-in before Louisa was in love with him; and he had not yet begun on the highlights before he declared himself passionately in love with Louisa. He did this one day when Louisa had lingered after a sitting to look at his work. The declaration was scarcely necessary. He was, as Josiah had said, a talented man. The portraits of the other four sisters were recognizable likenesses. Louisa's face, however, was of an unearthly, spiritual beauty, very much in the fashion just then, and could be recognized by no one except Herbert (for that was the painter's name) and Louisa herself.

When the other sisters heard the news, they embraced Louisa, and if they were disappointed they did their best not to show it. They continued to pose, although they now allowed themselves the luxury of an occasional fidget.

In due course young Herbert, elegantly dressed for the occasion, paid his visit to Josiah's study to ask for Louisa's hand.

*

At first he was nervous, but Josiah could not have done more to put him at his ease. He was given whisky and a cigar, he was pressed to take Josiah's own chair, and he was tactfully reminded of the social advantages of his social background by Josiah's inquiries after the health of his parents. Thus fortified, he came to the point.

'Of course you may have her,' said Josiah. 'Of course, my dear boy. Of course.'

'Thank you, sir,' said Herbert.

'With my blessings,' said Josiah.

'Thank you, sir,' said Herbert, and paused. He uncrossed his legs and crossed them again. 'That is ... I mean ... that is ... well, thank you very much, sir. For your blessings, I mean, sir.' He nervously cleared his throat.

'By that you mean, blessings and what else, eh?' said Josiah, with a wink and a nod.

'Well, sir, the fact is,' said Herbert, 'I am a little worried about the ... er ... well, sir, the "what else" as you put it, sir. I would like to keep Louisa in the style she's been accustomed to, and I'm sure I shall. In time, that is. You see, sir, a painter nowadays doesn't only need talent. If I've got talent, that is. I mean he needs ... ah ...' He blushed and took a pull at his whisky. 'Well, to be frank, he's got to cut a figure in society. He's got to have his studio in the right place, meet the right people, and so on and so forth. Then the commissions come in. But not otherwise. We English like to feel our artists are gentlemen, you see, sir.'

'And perfectly right, too,' said Josiah. 'A man wants to know a good deal about a man before he sends his wife and daughters to a man's house. Look at Raphael. I was reading about him only yesterday,' and Nottidge waved his hand towards an encyclopedia on his shelves. 'Perfect gentleman. Friend of the

Pope's. In and out of his palace every day. I don't hold with the Roman religion, but it stands to reason that a man cannot spend all the time rubbing shoulders with clergymen and be a wrong 'un. Or take Rembrandt – '

'Well,' said Herbert, hastily, 'there were one or two dubious things about him – '

'It's all gossip,' said Josiah. 'Pure gossip, you mark my words.'

'I'm sure you're right, sir,' said Herbert. 'People will gossip about painters, especially if they don't cut a figure. Rembrandt,' he said, slightly stressing the name, 'had no money.'

'Let me set your mind at rest,' said Josiah in a kindly voice. 'Louisa will bring you a house and furniture as a wedding gift from me, and a hundred a year.'

'A *hundred*,' said Herbert, and his mouth hung open in dismay underneath his aristocratic nose.

'Pin money,' said Josiah.

'I should say so,' said Herbert. Then recollecting his manners, he said: 'Of course, that's very kind of you. If I could add something to that out of my father's pocket – say, about nine hundred a year more, I'm sure we could tide over the first few years until I get some really good commissions. Unfortunately – '

'Unfortunately,' agreed Josiah, sympathetically shaking his head, 'Sir Thomas is a bankrupt.'

'That, sir, puts it in a word,' said Herbert.

Josiah poured himself some whisky with great deliberation. He then went to the bookcase, moved the encyclopedia, and revealed a safe. He unlocked this with a key from his watch-chain and took out a roll of parchment. He came back to Herbert, who had got to his feet.

'Young man,' he said, 'your father's a fine fellow.'

'Very fine, sir.'

'But he's got no sense of money.'

'It would rather seem so.'

'Now I have.'

'I'm sure of it, Mr Nottidge.'

'And I think you have, Herbert.'

'I hope so, sir.'

'Well, me lad,' said Nottidge, 'I'll tell y' something. I've got five unmarried daughters. When I die they'll all have a little something.' He paused. 'But I've left the bulk of my fortune — and I say bulk advisedly, Herbert — to one, just one of my sweet offspring. One,' he repeated, and cocked a bright eye at the now sweating suitor.

'Which one, sir?'

'*Aha!*' said Nottidge. He slowly unrolled the parchment under Herbert's nose. At the top were written in large, lawyer's flourishes: 'Last Will and Testament'.

'You're not a father, yet,' he went on, as Herbert, with popping eyes, read the engrossed script. 'You don't understand that I could never, never, hurt my other daughters' feelings by answering that question while I am still alive. But one it is that I've chosen for reasons,' he said in a fine baritone voice, 'that must remain locked in a father's heart. Here,' he said, more briskly, 'there's no hanky-panky. Here it is, all written out.'

Herbert peered. Herbert read. Herbert whistled, because it was a lot of money that was being left, in rotund but unmistakable language to ... to Josiah's left thumb, that was firmly clamped across the name of the golden woman that Josiah had chosen. Josiah snapped the roll closed. 'No hanky-panky,' he repeated. 'I swear to you by all that's holy I hope to be saved by the time my daughter's pouring all that money over her head, I swear to you, I'll never alter a word that's written on that parchment.' He looked at Herbert. 'Have some more whisky, my boy,' he said compassionately. 'Pour it out yourself.'

*

Herbert emerged from Josiah's study as shaken as the ensign had been. But before he met his betrothed he summoned up his breeding and was able to control himself. Only when Harriet asked when it would be suitable to call a little party of friends together to announce Louisa's engagement was there a moment of awkwardness. Herbert hesitated: he said he would like to consult his family about the matter, which was a well-judged remark. It reminded the sisters that they would soon be hobnobbing with people who had handles to their names, and that successfully deflected their attention for the rest of the evening.

The next day Herbert was far from his usual inspired self at the easel. He squinted uncertainly at his canvas and poked about among his colours with a preoccupied air. He bit his lip once or twice and then, with the manner of a man who has plucked up his courage, he announced that he felt he had done less than justice to the beauty of the other four sisters – the passion of a lover, he rather finely said, had overcome the passion of an artist – and he would like to begin the picture all over again. All five sisters were most agreeable to his doing so. Four of them because they felt that, on the matter of doing justice to them, he only spoke the truth, and Louisa because she was enchanted with the thought that his love for her had ruined a picture.

Herbert worked in an absorbed manner for the next two sittings, though he seemed to do more thinking than painting. Then he suddenly dashed down his brush in what Louisa thought was a very artistic manner, and exclaimed: 'Got it!'

That evening he sent Josiah a wicker-basket in which were two small Pomeranian pups. Round the neck of one was a prettily decorated label saying: 'For my dear Louisa'. Round the neck of the other was nothing at all. Josiah laughed so much at the puppies that his daughters began to fear that he was passing into his second childhood. He gave the second puppy to Agnes.

Herbert declared his passion for Agnes on the first opportunity, which was a butterfly hunt, a pastime just then becoming popular among young ladies. It was held in the neighbourhood of Sevenoaks, and Herbert chased a swallow-tail, or rather, Agnes, for a great distance. The butterfly escaped, but he caught Agnes. He drew her down to rest on a grassy bank and said that he loved her. Agnes blushed: she was the shyest of the family. Then she put up her face to be kissed because like all shy people, she was impulsive.

Herbert kissed her again and took her in his arms. He realized, as never before, that she was ten years older than Louisa, and that an artist's life was one of dedication.

'You're not surprised, Agnes?' he asked. 'I mean about my being untrue to Louisa?'

'No,' said Agnes. 'We've had something like this before and I've worked it out in my silly little head.' She essayed a simpering smile, and nestled closer. 'You see, five sisters is ever so many and I think we must be like Chinamen. Chinawomen, I mean. Chinagirls, that is. What *do* they call them, Herbert?'

'Never mind,' said Herbert. 'Why are you like Chinamen, Agnes?'

'Well, I think we must all look alike to strangers until they get to know us. Then you begin to know which is which. And what's what,' she said shyly, stroking Herbert's ear.

'That won't sound a very convincing explanation to your father,' said Herbert, aligning the conversation to more practical ends. 'I greatly admire your father. I'm sure you do, don't you?'

'He's all right,' said Agnes, without enthusiasm.

'But you love him, don't you?'

'Oh, yes. I suppose so. He smells of wood, sometimes, when he says good night. Then I like him. I like the smell of wood. Some woods, that is; some I don't. For instance – '

'*Yes*,' said Herbert firmly. 'But I'm sure your father loves you very dearly. The best of all his children, isn't it?'

Agnes did not answer.

'I mean, he gave you the puppy,' said Herbert.

'Oh *that*,' said Agnes. 'That's the first thing he's given me for years. He even forgot my birthday last September. Harriet had to remind him at the counting-house. He's never forgotten Harriet's birthday. She's the favourite. Oh yes, she's the favourite all right,' she said with a touch of sisterly sarcasm, quite unaware of what havoc her simple family phrase was doing. 'She always has been. She looks like poor mother before she died,' she said. 'Kiss me again.'

'The others will be wondering where we are,' said Herbert, privately reflecting that he, for his part, knew where he was for the first time for a week. 'Let us,' he said, perfunctorily patting Agnes's hair, 'keep our great love a secret.'

Difficulties melt before a man who knows exactly what he is doing, and Herbert soon found an occasion to be alone with Harriet. He sat on the sofa beside her as she did some household sewing. He talked of his career. He spoke of the importance of an artist marrying a sensible, experienced woman, as a corrective to his temperamental ways. When Harriet put down her sewing, he ventured to take her hand.

'Herbert,' said Harriet. 'When you speak of a sober, experienced woman, you mean me, don't you?'

'Yes, Harriet.'

'Herbert,' said Harriet, and resumed her sewing. 'I don't altogether approve of this modern fashion of having glass panels in doors. I suppose you, as an artist, like them, but I feel that there is nothing like good solid teak, especially in the house of a timber merchant. However, we do have a glass door to the conservatory. One day, a little while ago, it was ajar. You were working inside, Herbert, on the picture. Did I see you – I cannot be sure, with all that red and blue glass – did I see you counting off the five of us on your canvas and did I hear you saying: "Eeny, meeny, mo, out goes she"?'

She looked up from her sewing. She saw the young man's expression and she was merciful.

'I must have been mistaken,' she said. 'But still, perhaps people in glass houses shouldn't make proposals, Herbert, don't you think?'

Herbert did not come to the house the next day, nor the next nor the next. The painting stood, as lonely as Louisa, in the conservatory. Then one evening there was a loud clatter of hooves, a slamming of a hackney carriage door, the bell rang violently, and Herbert was shown in to Josiah's study. Louisa, peeping fearfully over the bannisters, saw that he was very unsteady on his feet.

After half an hour, he left. The carriage door slammed, the

horse clattered away, and the five sisters sat silently upstairs in their drawing-room.

Soon their father came up to them. He patted Louisa's head.

'He's not coming back, my dear,' he said. 'I am afraid he has got into bad company. These young sprigs do, you know. He was in no state to see you to say good-bye.'

'Did he,' said Louisa, bravely, 'leave a message?'

'No,' said Josiah. 'He talked mostly of horses. I am sorry to say he has been betting on them, and it has quite taken hold of him. He says that it is so simple. You put your money on the horse's nose – that's a racing expression, my dear – and win or lose, it's all over in twenty minutes.' He did not elaborate on this remark.

'And the engagement?' asked Harriet. 'Off, I take it, father?'

'Yes,' said Josiah. 'He asked me if he could break it and of course I said that he could.' He turned back to Louisa. 'You wouldn't want to marry a *gambler*, would you, my dear daughter?' he said.

*

The following morning Harriet suggested that it would be an excellent idea if they all went once again to Brighton: like all good housekeepers, she always aimed to establish a routine. All the sisters agreed with her except Cornelia, who contrived, in the instant, one of her passionate quarrels. She called Harriet a tyrant and a bully as usual, but when this was over, she got down to the knuckle-bone in a way not at all customary for her. She had been studying: it was true that the only books available to her were those from the Gentlewoman's Circulating Library, but with judicious choosing she had made that serve her purpose.

'If we listen to Harriet any more,' she said, 'we shall none of us ever get a lover. We expect men to come running after us. Some do. Eustace did. Herbert did. Need I say more? Eustace and Herbert weren't lovers. If we want lovers *we* shall have to chase the men. They don't mind it, you know. They rather expect it. You have to stalk them, slowly, slowly and lie doggo when they look up and sniff the wind, and play all sorts of tricks – and so do they, for the fun of the chase. And then, you pounce,' she said.

She put her hands in front of her like paws and gave a little jump. Her audience, that was listening to her with rapt attention, did likewise. Cornelia looked them over one by one and shook her head.

'But what happens to us?' she said. 'If a lover gets anywhere near us, he's got to face not one woman, but five,' she said. '*Five.* Imagine it. The poor man doesn't feel the joy of the chase: he feels he's being ruthlessly hunted down by beaters.'

That being so, she told them that she had no intention of going to Brighton with them. Instead she would go and join one of her aunts in Bath.

The notion of going to Bath struck the other sisters as a very good one, and such is the force of habit they all said they would come with her. They soon saw, however, that on this occasion, it would not do. They tried to think of other watering places to which they could separately go themselves, but they had few ideas, and even fewer aunts. In the end, Cornelia went to Bath, but the rest went to Brighton where they once more attended the meetings of Henry Prince and once more fell under that young clergyman's spell.

The aunt at Bath did not take her duties as a chaperone very seriously. She held that a woman of Cornelia's age, which was thirty, was quite capable of looking after herself. Cornelia was so capable that within seven days she received a proposal from a large, handsome and very masculine Irish horse-breeder, who was forty years old and looking for a good, steady wife to take back to Ireland. But within fourteen days Cornelia had so far looked after herself that she had been swept off her feet by an Italian count, to whom, in due course, she lost her maidenhood, the first of the five sisters to do so. She dismissed the horse-breeder, and doted on the count.

His name was Antonio Pansa. He did not look like Cornelia's notion of a count, because he had a snub nose and did not clean his finger-nails. But he had pretty eyes and charming manners, and Cornelia had begun, according to her theory, by stalking him. Her theory worked quite well, as we have seen, although the full excitement of the chase was necessarily lacking since the quarry came up and put its muzzle in her hand.

Cornelia's aunt warned her, conventionally, that she might be playing with fire. But Cornelia gave the matter her careful consideration and decided that she was safe. The Count had explained to her that he was a count in the Papal States. Cornelia had no idea where the Papal States might be, but she formed a mental picture of a countryside dotted with innumerable churches, incessantly ringing their bells, where young girls were either on their knees or herded into convents, and young men went in terror of their confessors. If the picture was unattractive, it was undeniably respectable. She felt as safe in his company as she would have done with someone who gave his home address as being in the close of Salisbury Cathedral.

She was deceived. She was deceived on several occasions, to her great content, until she was taken back to London by her indignant aunt.

Count Antonio Pansa followed her. He called at the house. Mercifully, there was no one there except Cornelia and the servants, her aunt having returned to Bath by the next train, thankful to have escaped explanations. When Josiah returned from Brighton with the rest of his family, he found an Italian count virtually waiting on his doorstep to ask him for the hand of his daughter.

While Cornelia, glowing, but discreet, made her explanations to her sisters upstairs, Josiah, also glowing, made his own explanations downstairs.

Josiah said he would be delighted to have a count in the family. He promised to give Cornelia a house and a hundred a year, and while the Count was struggling with his disappointment and the English language, Josiah produced the will. Josiah explained how he had left his money to one of his daughters, and, once more, he kept his thumb firmly over her name in the will.

The Count came clean. He had an elderly mother, seven idle

brothers, and three sisters waiting for dowries. He also had a castle in which, he frankly said, the rain came through the roof. From the proceeds of an unusually large crop of lemons, enough money had been scraped together to send him to Bath where, as everybody knew, there were hundreds of English heiresses longing to marry a title. Antonio said that he could see that Josiah was a business man; so was he, Count Antonio Pansa. He was sure that they could come to an understanding. Josiah replied that he felt most sympathetic: he felt that an heiress was only the due of a man with such responsibilities and one who had made such a long journey to get one. He pointed out that there *was* an heiress in the house, and invited the Count to call as often as he pleased. He then offered the Count the ritual whisky, which the Count, very green in the face, refused on the grounds that it always burned him as it went down. He accepted gratefully, however, several cups of strong black coffee. He left without seeing Cornelia, explaining that in aristocratic circles it was not thought proper after such an interview.

He saw her, however, next evening. Cornelia, a woman fulfilled, browbeat her sisters unmercifully. Without telling them that she had expected her lover, she packed off the entire family, Josiah included, to the opera. Once they were gone, she got rid of the servants by giving them money to go to a fairground. She spent a busy half an hour dressing herself in her finest negligee, and arranging the lamps in the drawing-room so that they gave a soft and patchy light. She opened the door to the Count herself. She drew him inside. She kissed him. An hour later the Count picked her up, and with only a word of assurance that the family were out, he carried her up to her bedroom.

Cornelia surrendered willingly to him, confident of once more tasting the delights of Bath. The count kissed her, if not with his usual passion, yet with care. The Count sighed. He kissed her again, even more deliberately, sighed, and began to kiss her yet a third time. He surveyed her charms, with concentration, sitting up on the side of the bed to do so.

Then he groaned. He took his head in his hands.

'It is no use,' he said. 'Every time I kiss I see here,' and he beat his brow, 'la mamma and my dear sisters, waiting and praying for their Nino to be a good boy and do his duty to his family and I am so very worried I cannot make love at all.'

He burst into tears.

The opera, being Italian and as unreliable as the Count, was very short. Josiah and his four daughters returned. They heard noises in the house and opened the door in alarm. As they did so, a slight, dishevelled figure burst its way through them and ran precipitately down the steps. At the top of the stairs stood Cornelia, magnificent in her rage and with no clothes on, throwing boots, shoes, pin-cushions and vanity boxes at the retreating figure of her disappointing lover.

Harriet, with a cry, ran upstairs, dodging the missiles, and covered her sister with a cloak. Josiah, after a single moment of incomprehension, sat upon a chair and laughed as he had never laughed in his life before.

*

Nor, indeed, was he to laugh so much again. That night he had a stroke, which enfeebled him so greatly that for two months he could not leave his bed.

When he at last got up, he was no longer the man he had been, and he was told by his doctor that he must resign himself to the fact that he might not have much longer to live. Josiah did not resign himself. He chafed, as well he might, for life had never been so delightful. He determined to enjoy what was left to him to the full, and he cast around in his mind for someone to follow the ensign, the painter and the count in helping him do so. He hit upon Prince.

One day he called Harriet to his study and asked her if she and her sisters would not like to invite the young clergyman who had so taken their fancy at Brighton for a stay in town.

Harriet said:

'Nothing would be more pleasant, father. That is to say, I'm sure it would be improving. But I am afraid it is impossible. He has a church of his own in Brighton, and I don't see how he could leave it. You will remember how full it was when you went there.'

Josiah grunted.

'Is it still full, Harriet?'

Harriet considered the matter.

'It was certainly not so full the last time we attended, father. I am afraid the people of Brighton are very fickle-minded.'

'You mean they've found another raree-show, eh?'

'That is unkind of you, father,' said Harriet. 'Mr Prince is a very sincere man.'

'I didn't say he wasn't,' said Josiah. 'The fact is, my dear, I think he's so sincere, I'd like to see him myself.'

'Yes, father,' said Harriet, with deep compassion, for this was the first time that her father had shown that he regarded his approaching end as solemnly as his daughters did.

'I am sure he would be a great spiritual comfort.'

Josiah sniffed noisily.

'About half full, would you say?' he asked.

'What, father?'

'His chapel.'

'Less than half, but the people of Brighton – '

'Yes, yes,' said Nottidge. 'Now be a good girl and get me my medicine.'

Left alone, Josiah thought for a while, and came to a decision. Had he known that his letter would arrive when Prince's hall was empty of all followers save one, he might have baited his hook with no more than ten guineas. As it was, he sent a hundred pounds. He sent it cheerfully. He was not, at heart, a mean man, because he was so very interested in money.

4

Martin Larkspur

PRINCE having promised Julia that he would spend thirty pounds of Nottidge's money in buying himself new clothes, they went up to London a few days before his appointment to see Josiah fell due. The day after their arrival, Julia took him from the inn where they were staying, in a cab, to a shop in Cheapside, near St Paul's.

'It's where I always take my brother,' she said, 'and I think he's very well turned out, and he hasn't got anything like your figure.'

The shop had a thick, bottle-glass window, through which nothing could be seen. Inside the floor was carpeted, the walls were panelled, and the decoration was in gothic taste. Altogether, the shop gave the impression of being the sacristy of some sybaritic monastery before the Dissolution.

Julia and Prince were instantly greeted by a man who blended the appearance of an archdeacon with the obsequiousness of a shopkeeper, a combination which was very much to Prince's taste. Julia said what they wanted and the archdeacon clapped his hands. Assistants, looking as much like monastic novices as they could in spite of having to wear trousers, came silently through what might have been a chapel door. They carried cards on which were painted clergymen attired with an elegance which was just this side of being sinful.

Prince studied them.

'Solomon in all his glory,' he said, 'was not arrayed like one of these.'

The archdeacon laughed a laugh as silver as his hair. But Prince caught the expression of one of the novices and understood that at one time or another in his life every clergyman who had ever come into the shop had made exactly the same joke. Prince was not abashed. It gave him a taste of the heady wine of being orthodox.

He studied one particular figure with care.

'Julia,' he said, 'I think that *that* is what I must look like to what Bunt calls 'the ladies'. Just imagine the effect of *him* reading The Song of Solomon to impressionable young women. Why,' he said, holding the card at arm's length, 'he looks as though he were capable of having written every word of it himself. Can I see something,' he said to the archdeacon, 'more expressive of the wrath to come.'

'Certainly, sir,' said the archdeacon, and he showed him a card which, for splendour, was to Prince's eyes identical with the one he held in his hand.

'I can see very little difference,' he said.

The archdeacon pointed here and there on the drawing with a delicate finger.

'The arrangement of the buttons, sir, is more severely rectangular in plan, while the drape, sir, although flattering, is less studied. This frock-coat, sir, gives the impression of being put on while the wearer's mind is on higher things. There is a sort of, how shall I say it, scholarly carelessness about it. We have sold quite a number to reverend gentlemen from the universities. But if I may make the suggestion, sir, perhaps in your case it would be better if you would be so kind as to place yourself entirely in my hands.' He ran his eye over Prince and sucked his teeth in the most delicate way. 'If you would be so kind as to stand up, sir, I could get a better . . .' he tailed off his words and Prince got up.

'There,' said Prince, 'what do you make of me? A university don?'

'No, sir.'

'A missionary?'

'Oh no, sir.'

'What then?'

'A reverend gentleman,' said the archdeacon, fixing his gaze on the shabby collar of Prince's frock-coat, 'who has until now been wholly absorbed in the spiritual side of his calling.'

'I regret to say,' said Prince, 'that you are perfectly right. As the Rector of my theological college always told me, "Prince, you will never make a bishop." '

The archdeacon coughed. He glanced at Julia; he sized up the situation in a moment and decided that Julia would be paying the bill. He ventured on a little impertinence.

'It would perhaps be difficult,' he said, 'in that coat. Will you step this way, sir?'

*

Three days later the clothes were delivered and Prince went to keep his appointment with Nottidge. He was shown first into the drawing-room. Here he sat for some fifteen minutes, surrounded by five women whose expressions reflected his splendour as clearly as though they had been the tailor's adjustable mirrors.

Harriet, Agnes, Clara and Louisa all wondered how they could ever have looked at their suitors, much less kissed them, while Cornelia, fighting back her tears, saw herself in a white veil kneeling at his feet and confessing her sins. When the maid-servant came in to say that their father was ready to see Prince and he rose to his feet, all the sisters rose as well, in a body. Prince fought back a desire to sit down again to see if they would all do the same. Instead, he bowed. They curtsied, Cornelia's curtsy being so low and humble that she had not recovered from it by the time that Prince had left the room.

Josiah Nottidge, however, did not rise. He sat huddled in a chair. His face was wan, the hand that he gave Prince to shake was thin and limp. But his eyes were as bright and sharp as a ferret's. The will lay ready, like a weapon, on the table beside his chair.

*

When Prince returned to the hotel and found Julia waiting for him in their room, he embraced her and kissed her tenderly.

'Thank heaven,' he said, 'that I am well and truly married to you. It has protected me from having a nervous breakdown and having, possibly, thirty thousand pounds in the bank. Josiah Nottidge, my dear, is one of the most unpleasant old rascals it has ever been my misfortune to meet.'

'Henry,' said Julia, 'then you did bite his head off.'

'On the contrary, he bit mine. He'd planned on my marrying one of his daughters. He didn't know that I was already married. I suppose he thought I was still – what did they call me, Julia? – ah, yes, the Kissing Curate.'

'Which one did he want you to marry?'

'He gave me the choice of the whole bunch. I could marry any of them I liked, so I gathered. But he'd left all his money to only one of them.'

'Which?'

'That's his secret. He won't tell.'

'Thirty thousand pounds, did you say, Henry?'

'More, possibly. Certainly its not less.'

'Oh Henry, how infuriating. We could draw lots, couldn't we?'

'What for?'

'To find the one who's got it.'

'Then what?'

'Oh,' said Julia, 'how silly of me. Of course, you're married already, aren't you, to me.'

Later that night, when she was endeavouring to step out of her voluminous skirt in the cramped, ill-lit bedroom, she sighed and said:

'Oh dear. I keep thinking of what we could do with that money.'

Henry, who was carefully folding his splendid clothes, said: 'So do I, my dear.'

'It seems so stupid. If only you were a Pasha, Henry, you could marry them all and keep them locked up in a harem, and then when that horrible old man died and went to hell for his wickedness, you'd be bound to hold the winning ticket, wouldn't you? Oh *damn*!' she said, as she ripped the hem of her skirt on her heel.

'Would you be jealous?' said Henry.

She did not answer for a while. Then she put her nightgown over her head and as she fought her way through it, she said:

'No, Henry ... I wouldn't be jealous, I think ... After all ... when I married the Kissing Curate I knew you'd be unfaithful to me, sooner or later. You never struck me, Henry, as a clergyman who ...' She got her head through the opening, smoothed her hair, and giggled, '... who had been wholly absorbed in the spiritual side of your calling.' She got into bed, and sat with her knees up, looking at her husband. He, too, was preparing to get into his nightgown. Such were the customs of the time that wives saw their husbands unclothed only for this brief, but unfortunately inevitable, moment of each day. He was, she thought, growing handsomer than ever. She said: 'No, Henry, I think I'd rather like it if you were a Pasha and I were your principal wife. I could keep all your other wives under my eye.' Henry got into bed. They lay for a while, side by side, looking at the ceiling.

'Thirty thousand pounds,' whispered Julia. 'There must be *some* way of getting it.'

Henry did not answer. But he lay awake for a long while, looking at the dim shape of his brand-new coat, and thinking.

'Keep them under my eye,' he said aloud, some twenty minutes later, 'that's it. That's what I've got to do. Somehow.'

'Yes, Henry,' Julia murmured drowsily, thinking he spoke of the money. 'We can have a strong box ... and keep it ... under'bed. Goo'night, Henry.'

'Good night, my dear.'

'Sleep well.'

'Yes, Julia.'

But he did not fall asleep till morning. In the long night hours he had laid a plan that was to change both of their lives.

*

While Julia was packing their trunk next morning for the return to Brighton, an elderly clerk arrived from Nottidge's office. He delivered a letter from Harriet, and a small

ather purse closed at the neck with a ring. When he had gone,
ince opened the purse and twenty-five gold sovereigns rolled
it on the bed.

He read the letter quickly.

'It's from the Five Signs,' he said. 'They want to make a thank
fering of their savings for my visit to them yesterday. It
ems,' he said, looking up from the letter, 'that I cast my
ock-coat on the waters and it came back at five quid a
ad.'

'Well,' said Julia. 'I'm glad they know the right thing to do.
ow pick up the money and put it in your pocket, Henry, and
urry or we shall miss the train.'

To travel by train was no longer a brand-new experience; but
e novelty of the station, the noise, the smoke, and the un-
miliar shape of the compartments had still not worn off, es-
ecially since the railways were constantly changing their
uge, their style and their rolling-stock.

Julia and Henry bought a first-class ticket, argued a little as to
hich of the available carriages would be safest in an accident,
d finally mounted the narrow steps of one of them, both Julia
d Henry a little flushed and excited.

Julia settled herself comfortably in one corner, and Henry in
other. Henry looked out of the window and his mind went
ack to his first rail journeys, and particularly to that which
ad taken him part of the way to and from Lampeter Theo-
ogical College. He remembered that he would sit in a carriage
or an hour, examining his conscience, as he had learned to do
the manuals of spiritual exercises. From habit, he began to do
again. He soon found himself studying his reflection in the
arriage window.

'Julia,' he said.

'Yes, Henry.'

'You were quite right about paying extra for the collar.' He
an his finger round the elaborately starched white bands that
arked him as a clergyman. 'Smooth as silk. How did you know
bout them?'

'I found them for my brother,' said Julia. 'He used to finish

76

morning service with a mark round his neck as though he had been hanged and cut down. It's always better to pay a little more and get the best.'

Prince resumed the study of his reflection, and of his conscience. After a few moments he found that he was staring into the face of a beggar hung with rags. The beggar moved his lips but what he said was lost in the noise of the railway station.

'Julia.'

'Yes, Henry.'

'I agree that it's always better to pay a little more and get the best. But isn't there something better still?'

'Perhaps for bishops, Henry. But I don't know where they shop.' ,

'I mean,' said Prince, 'wouldn't it have been a better thing – I'm merely asking, Julia – to have saved the money and used it – well, as I would say at the Adullam – to relieve the sufferings of the less fortunate? I repeat, I am only asking.'

Julia looked at Henry. She thought that his frock-coat, his shoes and his bands did her credit. He was more rewarding to dress than her brother, and if one took into account the Nottidge sisters' surprise gift (and in Julia's arithmetic, one did), the whole thing had cost no more than five pounds.

'Yes, Henry. It is always a good thing to give to the less fortunate,' she said. 'Give the man half a sovereign.'

Prince hesitated for she had named a sum twenty times bigger than what was normal to give. Then, searching his pocket, he produced the small gold coin, opened the carriage door and gave it to the beggar. The man, astonished, bounced up and down with delight. He took off his battered hat, and gave Prince a bow. Prince gravely returned it, at which the beggar, unable to repress himself, winked, made a gesture as of a man lifting a heavy tankard of beer, drank Prince's health in invisible alcohol, and then skipped off into the crowd.

Prince sat smiling to himself for a while. Then he said:

'Julia.'

'Yes, Henry.'

'D'you know, when I was at Lampeter a problem like that would have kept me up half the night.'

'What problem, Henry?'

'The problem of spending money on oneself, or giving it to the poor.'

'Well, so it should have kept you up. You hadn't got a half-sovereign to give, had you, then?'

'No, Julia.' And later. 'Julia, the next time I want to examine my conscience about such matters, I think I shall ask you to do it for me.'

'That's what the wives of great men are for,' she said. 'Look, I think that vulgar man is going to get into our carriage.'

*

If Prince had been feeling unduly proud of his new clothes, he was immediately mortified. The man who was standing by the carriage on the platform was so magnificently arrayed that had he walked on the stage of a morality play, all would have known at once that he portrayed the vice of Luxury. His top-hat was so high that it teetered every time he moved his head, and so ironed that it shot beams of light in all directions. His frock-coat was ample, rich and luxuriously curved in the lapels. His stock billowed and foamed like a frozen sea, in the depths of which was a pearl such as divers burst their lungs to find. His cuffs came down to his knuckles and were joined, it would seem, by jewelled fragments of a royal crown. Thick braid ran down the seams of his trousers, and from a pocket hung a fob as loaded with gold and enamel as a Spanish grandee's neck. Every-thing about him shone, and nothing more brightly than a pair of black, slight protruding eyes that were set on either side of a small and shapeless lump of nose. He caught Julia's eyes, raised his hat and gave a sharp, inelegant bow, while his eyes snapped brilliantly. He turned to Prince, and bowed again. Laying his curly top-hat on his richly suited right breast, he asked, through the open middle window, if he might join them. When they said that he might, he whipped open the door, leapt into the carriage with a twinkle of boots, swept aside his coat tails and sat on the edge of the seat, all in a moment. Placing two ringed hands on his knees, he gazed from Julia to Prince and from Prince to Julia as though he were a bird and they were succulent worms. While a porter, with great deference, placed a large leather bag beside him, he fixed his protruding eyes on a label on Prince's luggage. It was an old one, from Prince's early days, that had been too well glued down to remove.

'Forgive me,' he said, 'but have I the honour of addressing the Rector of Charlinch?'

'No,' said Prince.

'The Vicar, perhaps?'

'No,' said Prince.

'Ah!' said the man. He jingled his fob, looked Prince and Julia over with a stare which might have been insolent if he had not accompanied it with an expression of flattering approval. 'Ah,' he said again, and stopped jingling his fob. He had decided that the man must be in the missionary field. He suddenly sent his fingers flying into several pockets and produced, with another exclamation, a crocodile leather card case. The next instant, as though they were assisting at a conjuring performance Julia and Prince both found themselves holding large visiting cards, on which was printed 'Martin Larkspur' and an address.

'Allow me to introduce myself,' said the man. He sat back and scrutinized their luggage again, finding this time another label, and more to his purpose. He coughed, and drew his listeners' attention back to himself. 'As you see, I have the privilege of being a director of the London and Brighton Railway: this very line which will carry you in safety, comfort and in the fastest average speed of any railway in Great Britain, to your destination which will be, I take it, Brighton. Yes? Then I think you will be interested to know, sir, that we plan to erect there a new and even more commodious station in the very near future, which together with its shunting yards, station approach and quadruple passenger platforms will have a superficial area greater than that of Canterbury Cathedral itself, with all due respect, sir,' he added with a swift bow, 'to your cloth.'

Julia and Prince regarded him curiously. They both thought at first he had been drinking, but this was only one of the misunderstandings that all pioneers must endure. In less than a hundred years' time books would be written telling young men how to dress like Larkspur; lectures would be given telling young men how to talk like Larkspur; courses would be given at solemn seats of learning to teach young men how to think like Larkspur. Larkspur was a new sort of man; he was as new as the still gleaming wheels of the railway-carriage he sat in. He was the father of that forward-looking, optimistic progressive body of men without whom the glories of our own civilization would never have come to pass – the salesman.

Larkspur was very much aware that he was living in the Railway Age, as it was called, which, as everyone at the time said, was the most remarkable age in human history, not only because railways were being built as quickly as Parliament would pass enabling Acts, but because everything else was getting faster and bigger, and everybody was making more and more money. The whole nation felt buoyed up in a great wave of prosperity, and everybody was joining in the great, whirring, clanking business of making more and more goods faster and faster in an ever-increasing variety. In the factories, even little children were working fourteen hours a day. All this called for capital, more and more of it; so much, in fact, that business men sent out to raise it how and where they could. Larkspur was, therefore, aiming to sell Prince stock in a railway venture, for he had already, thus early in the history of such things, discovered that there is no easier victim than a clergyman with money to spare, especially if you can promise him that he will get rich quickly.

The guard blew his whistle.

'Ah,' said Larkspur. 'The guard blows his whistle.'

The engine puffed.

'Chuff, chuff, chuff,' said Larkspur, his bright expression growing even brighter.

'Right away,' called the guard.

'Right away,' said Larkspur, waving his arms perilously near Julia's hat.

The train moved off. The three passengers were flung backwards and forwards until all three were clutching one another.

'Acceleration,' said Larkspur. 'The fastest, smoothest acceleration, as proved by tests supervised by engineers of ours and rival lines, of any railway in the country. Listen to the wheels. Thumpety-thump, thumpety-thump, thumpety-thump: fifteen miles an hour already,' he said, triumphantly.

'Wonderful,' said Julia, pinning on her hat. 'And I've scarcely had time to pick myself up off the floor.'

Larkspur looked with bird-like glances from one to the other for a moment, meditating his next remark.

'You are an enthusiast, Mr Larkspur,' said Prince, politely, and was instantly overwhelmed.

*

'An enthusiast!' said Larkspur. 'The very word, Mr . . . ah . . .' He glanced at Prince's luggage again, 'Mr Prince, the very word that I would apply to myself. It is not often that one meets with such sympathetic understanding from gentlemen of your respected calling.' He went on emotionally. 'No, sir. They disapprove; they deplore; they preach sermons against railways. I do not understand it. I do not understand it at all. Consider, sir, what a tremendous help a railway can be in solving the problems of the church. What *is* the problem of the church, Mr Prince, organizationally speaking? Why, surely that there are not enough bishoprics, archdeaconries, rectorships and so forth and so on, to go round.'

'That,' said Prince, 'is undeniable.'

Confirmed, by this reply, in his opinion that Prince was a missionary, Larkspur said:

'Of course it is, my dear sir. But this is the Railway Age. The *Railway* Age, sir, and in the Railway Age all things are possible. Consider Africa, sir. Africa!' He sketched a map of Africa in the air, watching their faces closely as he did so.

'What have we in Africa? Jungles.' He screwed up his eyes and peered through imaginary lianas. 'Swamps.' He plodded in his immaculate shoes through ooze. 'Wild beasts.' He made his hand into claws. 'Howling savages.' He bared his teeth and rolled his eyes. 'And, sir, above all, above all, what? Spiritual darkness.' So nebulous a concept would seem to defy illustration, but he did very well. He held up his hands vertically in front of him, the palms outwards; he closed his eyes; he groped his way through a darkness so deep that, with no kindly light to guide him, it seemed inevitable he should be lost.

'But,' he said, briskly. 'We build a railway. We cut down the forest, we shoot the animals, we drain the swamps and one day the astonished savage leaning on his spear observes with round eyes the first steam locomotive drawing the first railway train into his one time fastnesses. Who will be the first man to alight, sir, from that train? Why, sir, who else but the Bishop-designate to the Dingo-Bongos, the Fuzzy-Wuzzies, the Mumbo-Jumbos. Just think of it! The vastness, the possibilities, the opportunities! Every two hundred miles of railway, a new diocese. I bow my head, sir, in reverential awe at the Christian possibilities, which the extension of the steamhauled railway train will bring in its wake.'

He paused, drew breath, and observing the expression on his listeners' faces, decided that it wasn't Africa; he would therefore try India.

'With all due respect to you, sir,' he resumed. I have always maintained that a railway train *is* a Christian. You smile, sir; you are sceptical, Mrs Prince. But hear me out. The world is full of evil, Mr Prince, if I may intrude on your professional territory, the world is full of the most terrible sins; unspeakable sins, Mrs Prince,' he added, 'though the one I am about to relate may be listened to by the gentler sex, not indeed without a shudder of horror, but without a blush. In India, madam, there is a savage custom among the Brahmini Hindoos, by which, when a married man dies, he is burned on a pyre, and on that pyre,' he put his hand in front of his eyes to shut out the sight, 'the unfortunate widow is compelled to fling herself – alive. If she does not, she is execrated. Why? Because it shows that the dead man was not loved, honoured and implicitly obeyed by his life's partner, a disgrace which is not to be thought of in those heathen parts. While we sit here, comfortably in a first-class carriage, bowling along at an unprecedented pace towards our destination, and sitting at our ease as though we were in our own drawing-rooms, who knows, sir, who knows, Mr Prince, that one poor woman is not, at this moment, expiring in unthinkable agonies.'

Suitably, at this moment, they passed through a tunnel. They emerged, their faces speckled with soot, into the light of day.

'But lo! we build a railway. An English railway, sir, built with English phlegm in the face of the fury of the Brahmini priests, with English contempt for their enraged wailings, their devil drums, their maledictions, and their devilish plots. We built it. It runs, to time, day in, day out. Now, say, a man dies. There is weeping, and gnashing of teeth. Small, wiry, brown men, their faces smeared with marks of mourning run to and fro building the pyre. In the women's quarters, if the term does not offend you Mrs Prince, sits the widow, surrounded by her relations, who prepare her for the dreadful ceremony. They leave her alone, to say her last prayers, to compose herself for the flames.' He paused. He glanced dramatically out of the window.

'But stay! What is that slender figure running down the road? Who is that woman, with heaving bosom, making desperately up the steps of the railway station? It cannot be, but it *is*, the widow. She catches her breath. She approaches the ticket window. She puts down, with trembling hands, her silver rupees, "A first class single to Khatmandu," she says: and she is saved. Saved, Mrs Prince, from a horrible death. For in Khatmandu she waits, a year, maybe two. The dead man's virtues are seen in a less splendid light, his vices are more distinctly remembered. No one feels, any more, jealous of his honour, and she returns to the bosom of her family to live to the end of her natural term of life, thanks to the railway. Can you deny now, sir, that the locomotive is a Christian?'

'You should put that question to the Bench of Bishops,' said

Prince. 'I am sure you would have no difficulty in convincing them that a locomotive is a Christian. As for me, I had considerable trouble convincing them that I was, but then I haven't your silver tongue.'

Larkspur took out a silk handkerchief and dried his forehead. By the time he had tucked it back into his pocket, he had decided that he had been barking up the wrong tree.

'But perhaps,' he said, suavely, 'you are not interested in the missionary field?'

'No,' said Prince.

'Not a rector, not a vicar, not a missionary,' said Larkspur to himself. 'He must be a crack-pot.'

'I am afraid,' he resumed, with a little laugh, 'that the Founder of Christianity Himself would have difficulty in convincing our bishops that he was a Christian.'

Larkspur paused to speculate upon the exact sort of crack-pottedness that Prince adhered to. It was difficult to decide; there were confusing factors. The cut of his jib was definitely Anglican, but then he was unsound in his views about bishops.

'You are, sir,' he ventured, 'an independent clergyman?'

'Highly independent.'

'Ah,' said Larkspur. 'You have, of course, a church of your own.'

'I have a following.'

'As yet, no church?'

Prince, divining the drift of Larkspur's remarks, said:

'As yet, no. But contributions are beginning to come in. A hundred pounds here, twenty-five pounds there. . . .' He observed the glitter that crept into Larkspur's eyes, and added, mischievously: 'And I have just been up to London, as a matter of fact, to talk to a businessman who is thinking of putting thirty thousand in my way.'

'A wonderful sign that heaven has blessed your work,' said Larkspur, fervently. 'You have accepted?'

'I have to consider the matter, Mr Larkspur. There are difficulties.'

'I quite understand. Yours is a strict creed, I have no doubt.'

'Oh no,' said Prince, struggling to suppress his laughter. 'Not at all. We are distinctly – ah – latitudinarian.'

That was all Larkspur needed. The pieces of the puzzle – the frock-coat, the lack of a cure of souls, the journey to Brighton, the business-man and the thirty thousand pounds – all fitted neatly together. He was talking to a fashionable revivalist preacher. He had met quite a number of them. They were his meat and drink.

'Let me shake your hand, sir,' he said, with emotion, and when Prince had allowed him to do so, he went on: 'I am but one of a great number of persons who are seeking, sir, for just such a man as yourself. I personally can think of scores of people, whom I count among my personal friends – influential people, well-to-do people – who hunger and thirst for a message which will go to their hearts. But it cannot be the old, tired stuff, sir. It cannot be sin and hell-fire and heaven-if-you're-lucky. This is a new age; a great age; the greatest that the world has ever seen. We are making all things new; is it wrong of us to expect that our faith should be new? I do not think so, and I think you do not think so either, sir. Are we *really* the sinners that they try to tell us we are from the pulpit? We, sir, we Englishmen of this unbelievable nineteenth century? Do we really feel sinners, men who should gnash their teeth and tear their garments? We, who are bringing, daily, such benefits to the world that generations to come will bless our name? No, sir. We may slip: we may have peccadilloes. But the great work that we are doing could not be done except with God's aid and we know it. God is not against us. He is for us, if only we learn to approach him the right way. As I have often said to myself,' he ended, eyeing Prince, 'if a new Messiah were to arrive on earth today, where would he arrive, sir, if not in England?'

It was at that moment, in a first-class carriage on the London to Brighton train, that Prince first saw his way clearly to his goal. Meantime, with Prince barely listening to him, Larkspur worked his discourse round to the business he had in hand.

Finally, he opened the bag at his side, took out a sheaf of papers, and said:

'... and that brings me to a scheme which has been specially designed for just such people – the backbone of the country as I was saying – who have neither money to burn but who, yet again, wish to take some part in this great crusade.

'It is a scheme connected with the extension of the railway network, and is, I may say, being heavily oversubscribed in the City of London at this very minute. But my co-directors and I have set aside a small block of shares specifically with the purpose of spreading the benefits which will flow from our venture to a wider section of the community than the narrow circles of London financiers. It is important for us, sir, to gain the goodwill not only of businessmen, but of the leaders of opinion in other walks of life.' He patted the documents in his hand and said: 'I wonder, sir, if you are interested?'

Prince pulled himself together. 'Mr Larkspur,' he said. 'I have never been more interested in my life.'

He took the prospectuses and pamphlets that Larkspur handed him one by one and read them with every appearance of interest, but Julia, watching him, saw with relief that his thoughts were far elsewhere.

So the time passed until they came to their destination. Prince, not to be rude, asked if he might keep the papers. Larkspur, with alacrity, said that he might. Larkspur looked out of the window.

'Never,' he said, sighing, 'has a journey passed so quickly, not even on the London and Brighton Railway, which holds the record in speed for any service run to a regular schedule. I am indeed sorry that we must part, Mr Prince, and, Mrs Prince, I hope I shall have the honour of meeting you again. Yes,' and he sighed again, 'I am deeply sorry we should part so soon.'

His sigh was convincing. He was regretting, as he always did, that in his field of business nothing in the way of money actually changed hands until long after, when the excitement of the chase had faded. He would have liked to carry off the golden sovereigns slung, so to speak, by their feet to a pole.

But this could not be, and he therefore handed Prince and Julia down from the carriage, raised his shining topper, bowed so that his magnificent fob jangled vertically from his stomach, and left them, a perfect gentleman, except for the fact that he could not restrain himself from pursing his lips and softly whistling a hymn.

5

How Prince Abolished Sin

As soon as Prince arrived in Brighton, he put the plan into action. Even while Julia was unpacking, and well before Mrs Cusack had recovered from the sight of his new 'clothes, he began searching for some means to keep the Nottidges under his eye.

He soon found them. A house next to the Adullam chapel was owned by someone willing to rent it to visitors. The owner, impressed alike by Prince's bustling manner and his new frock-coat, came to the conclusion that the Kissing Curate had fallen on his feet. He raised the figure that he had in mind for the rent, and Prince accepted it, provisionally. He had, Prince explained, to write to London.

He returned to his room and immediately wrote two letters. The first was to Josiah, the second was to the Misses Nottidge. He filled the first letter with pious platitudes and did not care whether Josiah read it or not. The second he marked 'Personal', to make sure that Josiah would.

In the letter to the sisters, Prince, having briefly called down blessings on their heads, went on to say how distressed he was to find their father in such a poor state of health. He wondered if the Brighton air would not do him good. There was a house available next to his chapel. It had a view of the sea. It would be very suitable but he supposed the ladies would never wish to cut themselves off from the gaiety and pleasures of the town.

He added a few courteous trivialities, a text and a pious admonition, and posted both letters. As he had foreseen, Nottidge, prying into his daughters' mail, made up his mind on the spot that his daughters would go down to Brighton if he had to drag them by the hair.

But he had no difficulty. Still dazzled by Prince's splendour, the sisters could think of nothing more desirable than living next door to so marvellous a man. All that is, save Cornelia. She said that she would not go. This was because of her changed position in the family, although she did not expressly say so.

Cornelia, of course, had lost her virtue to her Italian lover, and, of course, the family knew it. Had she been an only daughter, this would have caused dismay; but it did not greatly disturb the Nottidges. With five daughters, the chances that one of them would be, as the phrase went, 'ruined', were plainly large, and they had become accustomed to the idea that it might happen. They concealed Cornelia's slip from the outside world, of course, but otherwise did not persecute her. But Cornelia had given yet another hostage to Harriet. Cornelia might feel that she was the most experienced of the sisters, but she could not hope to be the most respected. This, as always, was Harriet, and, as always, Cornelia did not like it. She decided, therefore, that it would be better to be hanged as a sheep than a lamb, and said she would stay behind to mind the house.

Urged on, unnecessarily, by their father, the sisters wrote, over Harriet's signature, that they would be overjoyed to take the house. They would come, they said, within ten days. They told him about Cornelia remaining behind. Prince read the letter with satisfaction. He regretted Cornelia, but, as he said to Julia, it was four birds in hand, and they would have to put up with the fact that there was one in the bush. Besides, there was the hope that Cornelia might (he thought) feel lonely, and change her mind. What did worry him very much was that they left him so little time to do all that he had to do.

'What is that?' asked Julia. 'Getting the house in order? I've looked over it, my dear, and there's really nothing to be done. It is very comfortably furnished.'

'It's not their house that I propose to put in order,' said Prince. 'It's my own.'

With that, he begged to be excused from answering any more questions, and he shut himself up in his room for several days on end, emerging only for meals, and to send for more pens and paper. Julia heard him walking up and down hour by hour, and sometimes she heard the scratch of his quill as he wrote, or the rip of paper as he tore up what he had written. When he came out, he spoke only a few, preoccupied words. He explained once, at dinner, and shortly, what he was doing. He was founding, he said, a new religion. With that he fell silent and ate prodigiously.

*

It has been one of the most cherished illusions of mankind that it is possible, by taking careful thought, to give new meanings to the words Right and Wrong. The traditional notions are so simple, so dog-eared, and so dull that it seems beyond argument that in a changing world they can, and should be changed. The founders of most of the established faiths, however titanic their spirits may have been, never seem to have risen to this view. They generally agree with one another about the things it is right to do and the things which are not, and they generally agree, what is worse, with the opinion of the simplest old woman in the matter.

But Prince agreed with Larkspur. One of the first things he did to aid his meditation was to take a large sheet of paper and print Larkspur's name in large capitals on it. He then pinned it to the wall as a reminder, and set about his task.

His task needed boldness and courage. The re-examination of right and wrong every generation, or more often, with which we are familiar, had scarcely begun in Prince's time. He could not be sure where it would lead him. He hoped it would lead him to being a world-shaking prophet. In fact it led him to be the leading spirit in the Abode of Love, where he ended his days as a figure of comedy. It might, however, have led him to a much more grisly eminence. We can see this more easily today. We have Belsen, and crematoria, whips, light, boxes and bullets in the neck to remind us, besides those more terrible things that we can, but hope we shall not do.

But Prince's excursion into this field had the brightness and freshness of the springtime of the age of new moralities. It is pleasant, and it may even be profitable, to follow him at least along its first few steps.

In the first place Prince was quite out of patience with the religion of which he had been a minister. For a man who had done battle with two bishops and lost, that is not surprising. To find that a religion is not good enough for a person as clear-headed, as rational, and so forth, as oneself is tolerable. In a way it is a rather inspiriting feeling. But to be told, and by two bishops, that one is not good enough for a religion, is not in-spiriting at all. It is, in fact, scarcely to be borne by a man who has any proper pride: and of this last, Prince had more than his measure.

He examined his conscience. He would, perhaps, have been wiser to have kept his promise and left it to Julia; but he was now well launched on his argument, and time, if his plan was to be followed, pressed hard on his heels. What, then, had he done, to deserve his disgrace?

Here he took another piece of paper and wrote. 'The ladies', in large capitals. But when he had put this up on the wall facing that which bore the legend 'Larkspur', he took it down again, and wrote the less stark word 'Bunt'.

He was frank with himself, as people who are remaking our morals always are frank. Bunt, or as he put it Buntism, formed a part of his own personality. But then he owed it to himself to be as frank about other people. Was Buntism not part of everybody's personality, as well? Did it not form – he was no fool; he was no self-deceiver – did it not form part of the personalities of these women who hung about his lips and wrote him those interminable letters? Did he really believe that the Song of Solomon, which sent his audiences into raptures, was really only a symbol of this and that, and the other theological hair-splitting? Did he? What matter? Did *they*? That was the question, and the answer was that they certainly did not.

Yet were they not respectable people, as Larkspur said? They were. Buntism was as much a part of human nature as laughing or crying or those other things which are just as unmentionable in polite society as the longings of Matthew Bunt.

At this stage in his reasoning, he had a small truckle bed moved into his room and slept there: or rather, he dozed on his bed fitfully, for he was beginning to feel once more that enthusiasm which he had felt at the theological college and it would not let him sleep. Vast possibilities opened in front of him. He saw himself as the revealing prophet, the illuminator of dark places, the man to whom Providence had given a clearer vision of the truth than to other mortals. It is probable that nobody has thought of a new idea, however confused, without sharing, for a time, Prince's feelings, and for his time, Prince's idea was new. The recognition of Buntism has had a long history since then, and some voluble prophets.

Prince, after a large meal next day, and a little sobered, remembered that Buntism was all in St Paul. This cast him down, then buoyed him up. He could not be such a poor thinker, after all, if he had such a celebrated predecessor.

He gazed at the paper with Bunt's name on it once more. He ran over the hints of charges that the bishops had made against him, and the evidence to support them that fortunately was locked in his own conscience. Did he feel guilty? No. What harm had he done? He had created scandal, but what was scandal? It was offending the prejudices of men who, more often than not, never set foot inside a church but sent their wives to do their devotions for them. He dismissed the matter.

But why did he not feel guilty? Why? Was he stiff-necked? Certainly not; did a stiff-necked man examine himself in this meticulous manner? Was he – he must face it squarely – a bad man? He? If there had been more people like himself, who did harm to none, wished harm to none, and loved his neighbour as himself as much as he did, the world, he had to admit, would be a better place.

Yet why did he not feel guilty? Was it perhaps ... perhaps ... He hesitated on the verge of the tremendous thought but there was no denying its utterance. Was it perhaps that *in him*, it was not a sin, because *he* had been chosen by God for a special purpose, the awesome purpose of illustrating the truth of God's ways to Man?

*

For one whole day and night he did not come out from his room at all. Nothing interrupted the flow of his thoughts save, every few hours, the timid knock of Julia at the door, to assure herself that no harm came to him.

He said, later, that he had a vision, in which his mission had been gloriously ineffably confirmed. We need not doubt the fact that he passed some visionary hours in this climax of his long labours. He had been working feverishly for many days. He had been eating largely of Mrs Cusack's rich cooking, and a vision, is, after all, the only incontrovertible way of ending any religious argument.

The next day he emerged, ate breakfast, went outside, and took away the sign which named the hall 'The Adullam'. He returned to the house and dictated to Julia a series of letters to every one of the Lampeter Brethren and to every one of his disciples whose name and address was known to him. In terms adapted to each of the recipients, he summoned them to hear what he called The Great Declaration.

The first, and most difficult part of his plan had been completed, and in good time for the arrival of the Nottidges.

*

They came, and they were welcomed to their new house by Julia. It was at once clear that Josiah Nottidge was very weak indeed. He gave as much trouble as his feebleness would allow, and his complaints about the furnishing of the house, its price and its view were sufficiently vigorous to bring some colouring into his yellow face. But when he discovered that it was next to Prince's chapel he stopped complaining, and for a few minutes even smiled.

The sisters were busy attending to him, but they still found time to tell Julia that they were disappointed at not being met by Prince. Julia, with wifely loyalty, improved the occasion by telling them of the seclusion, the meditations, the spiritual exaltation of their idol, and she ended by handing them their own copies of Prince's summons. She improved the occasion so much that the sisters apologized most humbly for complaining. They read the summons in awed whispers and begged Julia to keep them front-row seats for the great occasion.

*

The great occasion was somewhat drawn out, although every instalment of it was impressive. The lengthening of the Declaration was due to two things. The Lampeter Brethren were slow in assembling. Some were busy curates, all had affairs of their own, and Prince, until now, had been fading from their memories as college friends do. The other cause was the pleasure that Prince took in his own oratory, and in this he was not being unduly vain. He had always been a persuasive speaker. Now he added to a compelling delivery, a sense of a great occasion. As the brethren and the disciples gathered, the hall grew fuller with each evening address, and the collection grew more and more impressive. Seeing the new faces, Prince unconsciously added the crowning touch to his art, the mark of all great orators in all ages. At the beginning of each evening he recapitulated, in short telling phrases, what he had said on the evenings before. After a week, this introduction came to resemble an incantation. It began with the phrase, spoken low and thrillingly: 'I am here to tell you, brothers and sisters, that sin must be pardoned in the conscience ere it is subdued in the heart.' As a beginning it was all the more impressive because Prince had ordered that there should be no hymns, no harmonium-playing, and even – a profoundly skilful touch – no prayers. The disciples gathered in silence: in silence, Prince, dressed in his London clothes, pale from his spiritual exertions and looking more beautiful than ever as a consequence, slowly mounted the platform. In silence he bent his head, then looked slowly over his lamplit audience. 'I am here to tell you' (the rich voice, controlled to the last vowel, seemed to supply all the missing music) 'that sin must be pardoned in the conscience, ere it is subdued in the heart.' The Nottidge sisters heard the phrase a dozen times. They never understood it – it is doubtful if anybody has ever done down to this day – but it always made them weep.

As the meetings went on, Prince, circling round his theme with profound oratorial effect, came nearer and nearer to the core of his Great Declaration. Although he was never so coarse as to put in so few words, it was, in substance, that God had made him a major revelation. The Christian dispensation was finished. All *that* was to be wound up. Christianity, its bishops, whether of Bath and Wells, Ely or anywhere else, had served their purpose. God had selected him, Henry James Prince, to be the perfect man, incapable of sin, and infallible.

Now most active and ambitious men have had something of the same sort of feeling about themselves, especially at the time when they have first emerged from financial deep waters and are beginning to find that life shows promise of being a little rosier. They also – though they do not necessarily attribute a divine origin to the feeling – are struck with the thought that they are not as other men are: they seem always to get the right end of the stick when others get the wrong one: they seem always to turn out right, and they are not – they are honestly not – conscious of having committed, or even wanting to commit a sin. But they get over it. They are perhaps unusually bumptious to their wives and their friends for a while, and overbearing to their subordinates, and then the thing passes, to return only, a ghost of itself, in their prosperous middle age, when they talk to the young, or to a mistress, or to themselves. They do not found religions, but they do found shipping lines, air lines, great commercial banks, industries, or pursuing a simpler path, become the leading statesmen of their country.

Prince, maybe, would have done the same if he had not gone to the Theological College. As it was he now gave ample evidence that he had not gone to a theological college for nothing.

The most obvious imperfection from which unregenerated

mankind suffers, is that people die. But Henry James Prince was perfect. Therefore Henry James Prince was immortal. This, Prince admitted, might sound unusual, but it was, really, the simple operation of cause and effect. Given that he, Prince, was without blemish, then he, the chosen one, would not die.

Prince may have felt that this bare announcement, while undoubtedly striking, was also smug. At any rate, he rapidly went on to tell his fascinated audience that those that had faith in him would not die either. This had not the benefit of the crushing logic behind the argument for his own immortality, but, for all that, it went down very well.

Prince passed on to the next of his privileges. He was, he said, sinless. Here his listeners, and particularly the Nottidge sisters, found him harder to follow, though even more intriguing. What Prince meant by being sinless was quite the reverse of the current view of that blessed state.

Prince was perfect; but Prince was not a spirit; he was made of flesh. Now the flesh has certain desires. One of these is called lust, and lust, except under narrowly defined restrictions which everyone knew, was a sinful thing. It was sinful, that is, with everybody but Prince. With him, to put it shortly it was quite all right.

It would be all right with his followers, too, provided, once again, they were strong in faith. In the matter of love between the sexes, both parties must be equally strong in faith; if they were, he assured them that they would be innocent of sin or even vulgarity. For the first time since the Fall of Man, fleshly pleasures could be enjoyed in an entirely spiritual way. In fact, they would not be fleshly pleasures at all. The flesh would be absorbed in the spirit.

All his followers welcomed this revelation thankfully, save one. The majority party could not have known, at that time, that their acquiescence was leading them straight into the Abode of Love. But, as it turned out, Prince had judged them correctly. They would not have minded even if they had known. The single objector was a young man called Rees.

Before he had become one of the Lampeter Brethren, Rees

had gone to sea as a sailor. This had left its mark on him. He was bluff in manner and frank in speech. He knew that starboard was starboard and port was port. He did not think that fleshly pleasures could be enjoyed in a spiritual manner. Prince, in his soft voice, agreed that they could not, in the normal way. It needed faith. Rees said he had faith. Prince, more mildly than ever, pointed out that he couldn't have, because here he was, contesting the decrees of heaven: or perhaps he didn't believe that Prince had had a revelation from On High?

There was nothing in the Manual of Seamanship to help poor Rees combat such subtle reasoning. Humiliated, he left the hall. The next day he resigned from the Brethren. Prince made no effort to stop him, and thus demonstrated that besides being attractive to women, he was a sound leader of men. He knew quite well that Rees should be sacrificed to strengthen the faith of the others.

Rees went north, and much later set up a church of his own in close connection with the Baptists, thus proving that, to put it at its lowest, he would have been a very uneasy member of the Abode of Love. We do not hear of him again.

*

The rest of the Brethren drew more closely round Prince, and to four of the closest Prince gave a special reward. He informed them that as their spiritual advisor he had found them four wives, all four of them sisters, and all four the daughters of a very rich and ailing man, and all four followers of himself.

When the Brethren had recovered from the surprise of this honour, they asked if the marriage that Prince proposed would be a spiritual, or a carnal one. Prince replied that first and foremost, of course, it was spiritual. But if any of the bridegrooms wished, it could also be carnal without in any way impairing its spirituality. He reminded them that sin was abolished.

Thus reassured, the four brethren joyfully acquiesced in their leader's wish and asked, although they had already guessed, the names of the chosen brides.

This would look like a hasty act on their parts, but before

they are dismissed as dupes, two things should be observed. First, it has been the custom in the larger part of mankind, during the greater part of history, for persons of refinement to marry women chosen for them by others, usually their fathers. Romantic marriages are a new, and as yet imperfect, system. The four Lampeter Brethren looked upon Prince not only as their father, but as their elder brother as well. Secondly, they were all four of them young men, who were never happier than when someone else was making their decisions for them. They rejoiced in submission and were only unhappy when nobody gave them orders to submit to. They would take most extraordinary pains to save themselves the trouble of thinking. They were the sort of people who, throughout the ages, at the behest of men who had the virtue of knowing their own minds, have enthusiastically become saints, criminals, heroes, or corpses.

The first of them, in closeness to Prince, was George Robinson Thomas, a clergyman of rather feminine good looks, who appeared always to be on the verge of saying something of great brilliance, but in fact never rose above chatter, which he could do, without ceasing, in two languages, English and French. Since he had spent some years in Paris, Prince sometimes called him 'Mossoo', and Thomas was very proud of this little distinction.

Lewis Price was the youngest and best-looking of the four. He was also in holy orders. He was willing to do as Prince told him in any matter connected with women, for he shared, in a watered fashion, Prince's attraction for them. But where Prince loved women in return, Lewis Price merely loved to be loved. His companion, William Puddy, admired him tremendously, as, indeed, he admired anything if he possibly could. He was, in many ways, the model of what the enemies of Christian love think a Christian is compelled by his tenets to be.

The last of the four was the most interesting. His name was William Cobbe and he was not by profession a clergyman, although he hoped to be. He was a member of a new profession, that of an engineer. He had taken a post on the London to Exeter railway, but unlike Larkspur, he had lost faith. The noise, the stink, the smoke, the unbearable people that he worked with, had convinced him that engines were the work of the devil. Uneasily surveying the prosperous and heartless world around him, he longed for the quiet pastures of a holy life; and he had, in any case, never been a very good engineer. He would today have gone into one of the many monasteries which are being run up, especially in the New World, to accommodate young men of his disposition. He understood less than any of the others what Prince was talking about, and he was the staunchest supporter of them all.

*

Having gathered in the bridegrooms, Prince next deployed the brides. A tea-party was held for the purpose in the Nottidge house, and Prince, having exercised all his charms for nearly an hour, suddenly told the sisters that he thought that they should marry. This, of course, was a disappointment to them, for it was something that everybody had been telling them ever since they had passed the age of seventeen.

But Prince went on to do what nobody else had done; he produced, at another tea-party, the husbands. He found no difficulty in negotiating so delicate an encounter; he peppered his conversation with quotations from the Song of Solomon and let the women take his meaning which way they wanted.

But this meeting was not as successful as he had hoped. There was some coldness on the part of the ladies and, as a result, considerable bashfulness on the part of the men.

That night, as they prepared for bed, Prince mentioned the matter to Julia. He asked her what she thought was wrong.

'Henry,' she said, as he got into bed and drew the curtains snugly round them, 'most of the time you are the cleverest man I have ever known, but sometimes you are quite the stupidest. The Signs won't mind marrying the Brethren, if you tell them that they ought to. But they'd all very much rather marry you. And I for one quite agree with them,' she said. 'Good night. We must sleep now because I have so much to do in the morning. How quickly things are happening these days! You are already

the talk of the town, my dear. I have been asked to three houses
which shut their doors on me when I became your wife. By the
way, Henry ...'

'Yes, Julia?'

'You will remember that I am your wife, won't you?'

'Yes, Julia.'

'Well, then, good night.'

*

Prince and his disciples, both male and female, were not only
the talk of Brighton, they were one of its principal attractions.
It was said on all sides that it would be a wondrously fine thing
if a religious revival could be known to have had its origin in
the resort. This was because the Prince Regent, long since King
George IV, long since dead, and long since forgotten save in
Brighton, had chosen that town for his frolics, or, as they now
seemed in a more respectable age, his disgusting debauches. His
pavilion still stood, as it stands today, as a reminder of his
fanciful bent of mind. The virtuous Victoria had closed the
place, but with a touch of her habitual contrariness, she had not
pulled it down. Another Prince, perhaps, not royal but less ig-
noble, could cover up its traditions by creating a more holy one
of his own.

Besides, many of the visitors were men of affairs, taking a
brief holiday from piling up fortunes: and such people prefer
their pleasures to be not so gay. They wish their minds to be
relaxed, but not distracted from what was their purpose in living
and their true delight, namely the pursuit of money. A touch of
the serious side of life, particularly if, like religion, it was a
serious side they were normally too busy to remember, suited
them admirably. They encouraged their wives to send the faithful invitation cards whenever they could. Clergymen were respectable guests and if there was a little gossip about their past,
it only added to their social attractions. Besides, their sober
tastes kept down the cost of entertainment.

Thus there were a great number of *soirées*, drives, excursions and the recently fashionable evening dinners, at which

Prince could put Julia's advice to good use. He managed to take the Nottidge sisters aside, one by one, and explain, as if to their ears alone, that he understood their dilemma.

He not only understood it, he could solve it. Whoever they married – why, even if they decided not to marry at all, he, Prince, would always consider them his spiritual wives: and since there was no sin, a spiritual wife was no different from a carnal wife, or a wife-in-the-flesh. Or to put it another way, a wife-in-the-flesh would be no different from a spiritual wife. Or to put it still another way, whenever the opportunity presented itself, he kissed them passionately.

*

The sisters now set about obeying Prince with a will. They organized carriage drives, and walks to the village of Rottingdean, and hunts on the beach for pretty shells to work into picture frames. The four incipient bridegrooms accompanied them on all these excursions, and often attended tea-parties and such in the Nottidge house. They sat with them during Prince's meetings and this was the most solemn bond of all.

Now that each sister knew that if she settled her choice on one of the young men, he would be, so to speak, only an auxiliary husband, they began to take a freer interest in their escorts' differing personalities. In due course, they began to sort into couples; gradually there was less and less confusion and drawing back when it was a question of who should get into a carriage with whom.

It was inevitable that Harriet took Lewis Price. She was the eldest, he was the best looking; he was also the nearest approach to Prince. Louisa at first was greatly attracted to the melancholy Cobbe. Since she was very young she felt that love was a very melancholy thing, and Cobbe's habitual mood suited her picture of a lover. But when he mourned over the vanities of life he was less to her liking: and when he talked to her of the beauties of contemplation, the charm of cloisters, the renunciation of the world, she felt that she was slipping, insensibly, into being a nun. She admired nuns greatly, but ever since the exciting and mysterious events of Cornelia's night with the Italian count, she had not wanted to be one.

But Cobbe suited Clara. She could not forget the unhappiness which Eustace had caused her. She had had her fill of the soldiery: Cobbe was a man of peace.

Shy Agnes blushed when any of them spoke to her, and hid behind her parasol. But she blushed the least with 'Mossoo', his manners were so easy, his Parisian tact so delicate. She thought his French very pretty, and certainly improper; but then, as she did not understand it she had no need to become embarrassed. As for his English conversation, unlike that of the others, it did not tax her mind. She flirted with him demurely. 'Mossoo', for his part, had less objection to her than to any of the rest, since she was quietly behaved. He responded politely to her advances, but no more. He was not in love; he had never been in love with anyone except Henry James Prince, and then only in the most exalted sense of that word. He would have been dismayed at the prospect of marriage, but he constantly reminded himself that he was doing it for Prince, and therefore was quite content.

That left William Puddy, and, once Clara had settled for Cobbe, it left Louisa. A word from Lewis Price as to Louisa's charms was enough to set Puddy head over heels with adoration. Louisa, like 'Mossoo', was content. She had, like him, fallen desperately and sincerely in love with Prince himself, but not in an exalted sense at all.

Old Josiah, meanwhile, got no better, but he got no worse. He kept to his bed, and grew even thinner. But whenever he heard men's voices downstairs, his black eyes grew so bright that he appeared to be striving to see through the floor, and he cocked his ears from side to side like a listening dog. Clerks who came down for a week-end to bring him papers to sign were bribed to spy upon his daughters; the nurse, a devotee of Prince's, refused to work for him any longer if he did not stop his questions. As for his daughters, they began to avoid his room, save at those times when he personally called them.

Josiah pieced together enough to know that there were no less than four suitors for his daughters, even although they denied, as yet, that there was even one. His sick brain feverishly busied itself with all the mischief that, with four lovers to play with, he could do. All night long in his mind, lovers and daughters danced up and down, through and round, and changing partners to his huge delight, but to the detriment of his ailing body.

*

Harriet wrote all this stirring news in letters to Cornelia, to which she received only the briefest replies, and sometimes no answer at all. Then one day, as Easter was approaching, she was flattered to receive a long letter from her sister in London, expressing the greatest interest in their spiritual adventures, and begging for more news.

Harriet liked writing letters; and nobody who has had a religious experience can refrain from spreading the light. Harriet wrote voluminously. If, reading over her letters, she had some doubts as to whether they explained things as well as she could have wished, Cornelia, it seemed, found them models of clarity. She read them aloud, she said, to the elderly cousin who had been called in as her chaperone. The elderly cousin, in a letter of her own, confirmed that this was so. Cornelia, she said, the dear good girl, read the letters to her of an evening while she was sitting by the lamp doing her sewing. She said that she did not understand everything about Mr Prince's teaching, but she was glad that the sisters were not wasting their time in frivolous amusements. She added, with unconscious skill, a touch which would go straight to any writer's heart. Cornelia, she said, always ran down to the door when she heard the post boy's knock and collected all the letters herself.

Harriet scribbled happily; and so did Cornelia. Then, one day when the lamp had been lit, the chaperone's sewing begun, and Harriet's letter opened, Cornelia suddenly gave a cry of dismay. The chaperone looked up to find Cornelia with her hand to her mouth, reading the letter with round eyes.

'Is there anything wrong, my dear?' asked the chaperone.

Cornelia nodded, swallowed hard and said: 'My poor dear

father has taken a turn for the worse. Harriet says I must come to him quickly before . . .' she paused, 'It is too late,' she whispered.

The servants were wakened, and boxes were packed in a respectful hush, and everything was made ready for Cornelia to leave as early as possible in the morning. Cornelia was distraught packing much more than the trip would seem to require. When the chaperone timidly pointed this out, Cornelia asked her, tragically, how she could know? Was she so sure that her poor dear father would die immediately? Abashed, the chaperone fell silent. Indeed, when Cornelia packed her jewelbox and said: 'My father always loved to see me wearing beautiful things; I shall put on my best frock and all my jewels and sit by his bed,' the chaperone, moved by the picture, burst into tears.

She was in tears, again, when she put her charge on the train. But Cornelia seemed to have gained control of herself. She was impatient to get to Brighton. She was, in fact, so impatient that she got off halfway, at Reigate. There she was joyfully met by a handsome man with curling chestnut hair, who drove her and her boxes away in a hackney carriage.

*

A week later, Harriet, Clara, Agnes and Louisa returned from a walk along the promenade in the happiest spirits. The sun had shone: the air had been soft; their gentlemen friends had discussed theology, it was true, but with several gay touches, and once, on the cliffs, had been positively worldly in their jokes. Harriet went upstairs to see Josiah and returned with the news that he was much as usual, and that his current grumble was only about his pillows. They went into the drawing-room for tea, chattering happily, and Harriet was delighted to see a letter addressed to her in Cornelia's handwriting lying on the silver plate which the maidservant held out to her. She had not heard from her sister for several days, and she opened the letter eagerly. She noted that it was long and she supposed that Cornelia was making up for her neglect.

A little later she put the letter slowly down on her lap.

'And how is our dear sister?' asked Clara, yawning, for this correspondence had begun to bore them all, save Harriet.

Harriet glanced at the maidservant. She waited, silently, until she had left the room.

Then she said, 'Cornelia has eloped. She has married an Irish horse-breeder.'

Clara was the first to regain her voice.

'Did you say "married"?' she asked.

'Married,' said Harriet, implacably. 'In church.'

Clara, Agnes and Louisa avoided one another's eyes. All were thinking the same thing, and all knew it. They had thought that they could suffer no worse pangs than those they had endured when they lost their lovers. But the pangs they felt because Cornelia had kept one were far, far worse.

'I shall read you her letter,' said Harriet. 'She begins: "Dear Harriet, I'd better warn you that if you're expecting that this letter is going to be full of pious drivel like the others you are due for a shock. So all of you hold on tight to your curates' hands. I'm married – and to a man." '

Harriet laid the letter on her knees for a moment.

'She puts the last word in large capital letters,' she said. 'Excessively large letters.'

'What does she mean by that?' asked Louisa, jutting out her chin. 'What else does anybody marry?'

'Curates,' said Clara, bitterly. And then, with considerable venom, she said: 'Cornelia always was a vulgar little bitch. Where did she find this prize-fighter Harriet?'

'Horse-breeder,' said Harriet. 'She says she met him at Bath. He'd come over from Ireland specially to find a wife. Cornelia says it was practically love at first sight.'

'Oh?' said Clara. 'Love at first sight, was it? And what was Cornelia doing when he saw her to produce *that* effect, may I ask? Vaulting on and off a horse stark naked, I suppose.'

'Control yourself, Clara,' said Harriet. 'I know how you feel, but after all, we must remember that Cornelia has only done what we would all like to do if we had the chance.'

It was an unfortunate remark. Clara dashed her tea-cup on to its saucer and rounded on her sister.

'If you think that I'd marry a horse-breeder, let me tell you, sister darling, that you're talking through your bun.'

'But, Clara,' said Harriet, taken aback by the violence she had aroused, 'Cornelia doesn't have to breed the horses. And it's quite a respectable profession.'

'She'll have a horrible life,' said Agnes, in a hollow voice. 'She'll be up night after night sitting on mares' heads while they have foals. I know. I read a book about it.'

'She obviously doesn't think much of him,' said Louisa. 'Look at the sneaking way she's got married.'

'I'm afraid it's us she doesn't think much of,' said Harriet. She says. "Patrick is handsome and he's got big shoulders and a wonderful smile. He's not the clever sort, except with horses, and I knew what would happen if you and Clara and Agnes and Louisa caught sight of him. Patrick would have been driven frantic with all of you baying at his heels like a pack of dogs." '

'I'll dog her when I see her,' said Clara, 'I'll smack her face.'

'I don't think she means to be as insulting as she sounds,' said Harriet. 'I think she's just picked up a horsey way of talking. She always was impressionable, you know. Look how foreignly she behaved when she met that Italian.'

'Well,' said Agnes, bitingly, 'she hasn't been as quick a learner this time. You don't call them dogs, you call them 'hounds'. To call them dogs is worse than kicking them in the ribs. I suppose he's letting her say "dogs" now, because it's their honeymoon, but if she does it after that I dare say he'll beat her black and blue.'

Clara, after contemplating this picture for a moment, found it so inspiring that she said:

'Well, *I say*, let's all have another cup of tea.' She busied herself with the spirit-stove, the kettle, the teapot and the caddy, making a defiantly cheerful rattle, over which Harriet read the rest of the letter.

It appeared, through the clatter of tea-things, that Cornelia had told Patrick that her father would never consent to the marriage and Patrick, who had long ago written to her that he wanted her for himself alone, suggested that they eloped. So they had done so, and been married in Clonmel. Cornelia said there were all sorts of exciting things she would like to tell them about married life but she was not sure that they were quite the right things to discuss with maiden ladies: or, she added, the prospective brides of clergymen. She asked, finally, about her father's health, and begged Harriet to break the news gently. 'He can cut me out of the will, if it will give the dear old man any pleasure,' she said. 'Patrick has fifteen hundred acres.'

'Of bog,' said Clara.

'She goes on to say,' said Harriet, steadying her voice, ' "and Patrick has a house in Dublin, on Trinity Green, and I'm going to be presented to the Governor-General up at the Castle on the next Queen's Birthday. Your affectionate sister, Cornelia." ' She folded the letter carefully and put it into the pocket of her dress. She surveyed the faces of her sisters as they digested this last, bitter morsel. Suddenly, she warmed towards them. Years of being the head of the house fell from her, Cornelia, had, after all, struck at her more than any of them.

'You must remember, girls,' she said in a voice that none of them could remember her using before 'that when Cornelia was twelve years old, father whipped her very, very hard for being a beastly little liar.'

*

The lamps were brought in; Clara, Agnes and Louisa went upstairs to dress for Prince's evening meeting, but Harriet sat alone for a while. Then she rose with the air of a woman who had made up her mind. She went upstairs to Josiah's room.

She found him greedily ladling soup from a bowl into his mouth.

'Good evening, father,' she said.

'Go away, Harriet. I'm eating my soup,' said the old man.

'I'm glad to see you're enjoying it, father.'

'Eh?' he said. He glanced up at her, a trickle of soup running down his chin. 'There's plenty of life in the old dog yet,' he said.

'I'm sure there is,' said Harriet. 'Nobody wants you to die, father.'

'Die?' said Josiah. 'Die? Who talked of dying? That's a fine thing for a daughter to do. Come into a sick man's bedroom and talk of dying. I suppose you want to get rid of me so that you can throw my money away on your fancy curate, eh? Take this damned dishwater away,' he said to the nurse, 'and don't come bothering me till I ring for you.'

Harriet walked to the window and looked out into the darkness.

'Father,' she said, 'have you any objection to Mr Prince?'

'I didn't say I had and I didn't say I hadn't,' said the old man. He banged his pillows, and feebly tried to adjust them. Harriet, most unusually, did not move to help him.

'Or the others?' she went on. 'Do you have any objection to them, father?'

'Haven't met 'em,' said the old man. 'Haven't seen 'em.'

'They've all visited you several times, father.'

'Not to talk to,' said Josiah. 'Not to talk to.' Harriet turned quickly. She saw Josiah's eyes, bright in the lamplight, and all the brighter for the pallor of his cheeks.

'Father,' she said, 'I have often wondered what you said to Eustace, and Herbert, and that poor Italian.'

'What do you mean, "said"?'

'I don't know. I only know that they were all of them happy before they spoke to you, and there was nothing but trouble afterwards.'

'You noticed that, did you, eh? And I suppose you want to blame it on me?' said Josiah.

'Yes.'

Josiah gave her a penetrating stare.

'Did any of them ever say a word against me?'

'No.'

'Did they say I was mean, eh? About money, eh?'

'No. They said,' said Harriet, slowly, 'that you were generous.'

'Aha!' said the old man. 'They said that, did they? Well, they were right, my girl. I've been a loving father to you all, and I told 'em I'd go on being one. Ask your fancy curates to come and see me for a nice, long chat, and I'll tell them the same.'

'I won't, father.'

'You won't, Harriet? You don't say "won't" to your father.'

'I do this time, father, because I think – I *think* – I know what you'll say to them.'

She moved towards the door. The old man eyed her cautiously, but said nothing. She bent over him, smoothed his pillows, and brushed back his thin hair with her fingers.

'Is there anything you want, father?'

'No.'

'Then I'll go off for the meeting.'

' "Me beloved's like a heap of wheat; me beloved's like a turtle dove," ' said Josiah, through his nose in what he deemed to be an imitation of Prince reading from the Song of Songs. He chuckled weakly.

'Yes,' said Harriet. She took the letter from her pocket and put it carefully into her father's bony hands. 'That's a letter from Cornelia,' she said, speaking clearly and slowly. 'She's run away from home. She's eloped with an Irish horse-breeder and she's already married.'

*

A little later, downstairs, she said to the nurse:

'I think you had better go up and see Mr Nottidge.'

'He didn't ring, ma'am,' said the nurse.

'I don't really think he *can* ring,' said Harriet, calmly. 'He seems to have taken a turn for the worse. I shall go and fetch the doctor, and then I shall go on to the meeting. If I am wanted, I can be called,' she said, then, unhurriedly, she put on her hat and her gloves, and left the house.

*

That night, although he had given a particularly impassioned address, Henry Prince left the meeting-hall with a jaunty step. He took his wife's arm and led her across the road to their lodgings, humming a little tune. He shouted a cheerful good-night into the landlady's parlour, and climbed the steps two at a time. When they got to their bedroom he threw off his frock-coat, and then, seizing Julia by the waist, pulled her into a little hopping dance. Julia, laughing, tripped and sat on the bed.

'Well,' she said, 'and what did the Five Signs have to say to you after the meeting? I was longing to hear, but I was caught by Mrs Earnley again. That woman is quite determined to have a harpist open the meetings. It'll turn out she plays the thing herself and looks queenly while she's doing it. I think we might let her . . .'

'Four Signs, not Five,' said Prince. 'And, by the way, the Sign that stayed in London has had a runaway marriage with a jockey.'

'No! A jockey?'

'Something like that. They were all talking at once, and I didn't get the details. But it doesn't matter. *She* won't get the money. The old scoundrel has taken it very badly and I'll bet he'll cut her out of the will as soon as he's able to speak. The important thing is that the other Four Signs are falling over themselves to get married. I think they feel, after the jockey or whatever he is, if they remain spinsters any longer the shame will be too much for them to bear. They want to get engaged. "Betrothed", they call it.'

'That's what you call it yourself, Henry, in your sermons.'

'So I do. "Betrothed",' he said in his most beautiful voice. ' "Betrothed". Bunt wants to make a moving little ceremony out of it.'

'Why not let him do it?' said Julia. 'He's been so useful about the place. We owe it to him to let him have his own way.'

'Just as you like, my dear,' said Prince. He took off one shoe. He straightened up. 'Four,' he said. He raised his arms as though he aimed a sporting gun. 'Pop, pop, pop, pop! Four little birdies and we don't even have to worry about the one in the bush.'

There was a knock at the door.

'Hush, dear,' said Julia. 'It's the landlady with your hot choco-late.'

'Chocolate,' said Prince, sticking out his lower lip like a recalcitrant small boy. 'I don't want any chocolate. I want some champagne.'

'All in good time,' said Julia, and, rising, opened the door. She took the two cups from the landlady, who threw Prince a languishing look.

'Good night, sir,' said the landlady, sighing. 'I'd just like to say that I thought you were beautiful tonight, sir. Really beautiful, I did.'

'Thank you,' said Prince. 'Thank you very much.'

From habit, he returned the look, and sent the landlady off to bed a happy woman.

He grimaced as he sipped the chocolate.

'So now,' said Julia, 'I suppose you'll have five wives.'

'Eh?'

'Spiritually, of course.'

'Oh, yes!' said Prince, laughing and spilling his chocolate. 'Oh yes, of course. Five wives. I shall call you all by the days of the week so you will know when you have to come to your lord and master's bedchamber.'

'Yes,' said Julia. 'That will be very tidy.' She warmed her hands on the cup of chocolate for a moment, looking away from Prince.

'Henry,' she said.

'Yes, Julia.'

'I hope . . .' she paused. 'Oh well, never mind.'

'But what were you going to say, Julia?'

'Me? Oh . . . I just wanted to say', she said, imitating the landlady's voice, 'that "I thought you were beautiful tonight, sir, really beautiful, I did". And I still do,' she said, softly, in her own voice. Then after a moment she sadly finished:

'And I think, heaven help me, I always shall.'

6

Love and Money

On the morning of the day that had been chosen for the announcement of the quadruple engagement, Prince, going across to the meeting-hall to search for a book he had left there, found Sergeant Bunt in his shirt-sleeves surrounded by great baskets of flowers. On Prince's preaching table were a dozen flower vases, and more vases stood on chairs, on the platform, and in convenient nooks in the panelling. Bunt was arranging the flowers in the vases, puffing and grunting a little as he bent down to choose them from the baskets at his feet, but, for all that, filling the vases with surprising delicacy. He held each flower between finger and thumb; he surveyed it with his eyes half-closed; he inserted it into the vase and then stepped back to admire the effect. When each vase was full he placed it carefully in an effective position on the platform, and stepped back once more to admire it over the expanse of his paunch.

Prince stood under the gallery by the stove for a while, watching him. Then he coughed, and came forward. Bunt gave a start and then said, a little shyly:

'Ah, good morning, sir. I was just doing the flowers. Mrs Prince said I might.'

'Good morning, Bunt. You're doing them most artistically. But then you are an artist, aren't you, Bunt? I remember how you frescoed that cave.'

Bunt reddened. 'Now, sir,' he said sheepishly, 'you mustn't go on twitting me about that, sir. It's all behind me, Mr Prince. Since listening to you I feel a new man. Quite reborn, sir, as you might say.'

His red, round face, the wisp of hair which, loosened by his exertions, curled up over his forehead, and the flowers he clutched in his hand, did, as Prince observed, give him the appearance of a huge infant who had just run in from playing on some gargantuan meadow. But this illusion quickly disappeared with his next words.

'I love engagements,' he said. 'I like them better than weddings. I get coarse thoughts at weddings. So does everyone else if they'd only own up to it. But there's not so much of the old Adam, if you'll allow me to say so, about an engagement. An engagement makes me think of lambs and spring and true-lovers'-knots which is very refreshing for a man of my disposition.'

'Strictly speaking, Bunt, there's no old Adam at all about this engagement. Our Brothers and Sisters in our little community cannot sin, provided they believe, Bunt. You follow me?'

'Ay, ay, sir,' said Bunt.

'So logically, all we need among ourselves is for the brother to get up with the sister in question and declare that he intends to take her for his wife.' Prince eyed the flowers. 'At least, that was my notion of the occasion. Something rather austere, Bunt.'

'No ceremony, sir?' asked Bunt, anxiously.

'I hadn't thought of having one, Bunt, no.'

Bunt shook his head doubtfully.

'But you think that there should be, Sergeant?' asked Prince, seating himself on one of the hall chairs.

'It's not for a man like me to disagree with a man of your education, sir,' said Bunt.

'On the contrary, Sergeant. I have always found you an education in yourself. Go ahead with the flowers and give me the benefit of your ideas on the subject, Bunt. I am all attention.'

'Well, sir,' said Bunt, resuming his delicate task with the vases, 'looking down at things from the lofty heights of your intellect, sir, a ceremony isn't strictly necessary. But we lower mortals, sir, stand in need of a little something to keep us respectable. People put great store by it, sir, as I remember Mr and Mrs Riggs found out to their cost, Mr Prince. Of course Mr and Mrs Riggs were only common or garden missionaries, and not to be mentioned in the same breath as yourself who has brought us all a new revelation, but when I've heard you speak, sir, of sin being abolished between us fortunate ones, many's the time that

I've said to myself, "Mr and Mrs Riggs". It's a warning, sir, what happened to them, and no mistake.'

'Who are they, Bunt?'

'Mr and Mrs Riggs, sir? Mr and Mrs Riggs are two godly and upright souls, man and wife, that I happened to meet when I was wandering in the outer darkness, before I came to you, sir. Mr and Mrs Riggs were wandering in the outer darkness, too, though it wasn't for any fault of their own, not to my way of thinking.'

He bit off the end of a stalk, spat it out on the platform, and, with his little finger crooked, set the flower with finesse into the vase among its companions.

'They were missionaries, as I said, Mr Prince. They were sent out to spread the Gospel among the heathen and they did it, more's the credit to them, until the heathen sent them back with, if you'll excuse the coarse expression, a flea in their ear.

'They were sent to a place which they don't care to name these days,' he went on, 'and with good reason. But I'd not be very surprised if it was in the same waters as the place where I had my own little misfortune. It sounded very like when Mr Riggs told me about it, but I didn't want to press the question for fear of looking nosey. Anyway, sir, it was a fine, warm place, full of heathens who'd never seen a white man before except to row out to a ship once a year or so and swap coral and pearls and such like for penknives and Lancashire cotton. No. There I stand corrected, Mr Prince. They had no use for Lancashire cotton, because they went stark naked except for some beads – for the ladies – and a small piece of bark – for the gentlemen. A very remarkable costume, no doubt you're thinking, and so did I the first time I saw something of the sort myself, but it's a strange thing how quickly you get used to it. More's the pity.'

Bunt sighed. He took the flowers out of the vase with a pettish exclamation, and began his arrangement again.

'Well, Mr and Mrs Riggs were sent out to this place by their Society here in London with instructions to do what they could to bring the light to these heathens and a ship would call again for them in a year's time to the day, weather and funds permitting.

'It all started off very happily, and Mr Riggs had tears in his eyes when he told me of it. The ship anchored, and the heathen swam out, laughing and shouting and splashing, and climbed aboard, all dripping wet.' Bunt paused. 'Very pretty, it is, sir. I've seen it myself,' he said, a distant look in his eyes, 'many a time. Unlike Mrs Riggs,' he resumed, 'who'd never seen the like in her born days, and didn't know where to look, as she told me herself, except up at the mizzen-mast, which is tiring on the neck. Anyhow, the captain had a few words with the heathen, and so did Mr Riggs – and a very few words they were because the heathen spoke a language practically all their own. Then out came the penknives and the looking-glasses and the upshot of it all was that Mr and Mrs Riggs were rowed ashore, while Mrs Riggs, as a temporary measure, in a manner of speaking, kept her eyes shut.

'The heathen soon built them a little house, and brought ashore the stores – those they didn't drop in the water, for they're a careless lot, in those parts, as I can bear witness myself. Then the ship sailed away for England, Home and Beauty. Mr Riggs was a bit homesick, of his own admission, but Mrs Riggs had got quite settled in and had taken a liking to the place. As I say, it's surprising how quickly you get used to things.

'But not everything. There was something Mrs Riggs could never get used to. I don't quite know how to put this, Mr Prince, to a gentleman in holy orders like yourself. But if sin is abolished among our little community – as it is, sir, I agree – then you might say that sin had never even arrived in theirs. Am I correct, sir, as to my theology there?'

'I doubt it, Bunt,' said Prince. 'But please go on. I am anxious to know what new trial Mrs Riggs had to suffer.'

'Trial you may well call it,' said Bunt. 'According to the Riggses, and I have every reason to believe them, those heathen had no idea of what you might call the conventions at all, sir. If they had any form of marriage, the Riggses never came across it. But as for what I shall call, respectfully, the joys of matrimony, the Riggses hardly came across anything else. It got so that Mrs Riggs could scarcely go for a walk of an evening for fear of seeing something going on in the bushes that no respectable lady would wish to come upon. Loving couples, sir, to call a spade a spade, littered that island, the heathen having no morality worth speaking about, except an old man, who was a sort of king, and who settled any quarrels, and kept the children in order with a stick. Nobody else did. The island swarmed with little darlings who you might call orphans and then again you might not. They had a mama and a papa, each of them, because it is the way that God has designed things for us here below; and I'm sorry to say, sir, it was God alone who knew who their papas were. Even their mothers were a bit on the vague side after the little ones learned to walk.

'As Mr Riggs said, it was a scandalous state of affairs, but then, as Mrs Riggs said, it was going to take a lot of ground work to make them see it. But Mr and Mrs Riggs fought the good fight and Mrs Riggs took her constitutional along a well-beaten track where she didn't need a lantern, and they both set about learning the language, with the object, of course, of bringing home to them what dreadful things were going on.

'As soon as they learned enough to ask questions and understand the answers they learned about one of the customs of the island which, seeing as how I'm very fond of flowers, as you may have noticed, Mr Prince, I have rather a weakness for. The custom, sir, was this. When a young man began to feel amorous sentiments towards a young lady, he went into the forest and picked a flower. He stuck this flower in his hair and went to find the lady he was setting his cap at, or, as I should say, since they didn't wear caps, his flower. The young man, with the flower in his hair, if you follow me, sat down beside his prospective fiancée and looked at her in a significant way. This look – Mr Riggs didn't describe it in any detail, but I suppose it might be described pretty safely, as a yearning look – this look was understood by all and sundry and in particular by the young lady as meaning, "I think you are beautiful and I want to make love to you before this flower in my hair is withered." Or words to that effect. If the young lady is agreeable to the proposition, she gets up, goes into the forest and finds the same flower which she likewise puts into her hair. And very pretty it must look too, judging from my own observations in those parts, for there's no denying it, if you like black hair, to which myself I am rather partial, they've got the best heads of black hair you'll come across in a twelve month cruise. Well, sir, down she sits by the young man and gives him a look, which is also understood to mean, "I think you are a fine fellow-me-lad, and I would like you to make love to me before this flower fades that I have in my hair." Almost poetry, isn't it?

'Well, then,' he said, giving the daffodil a toss, 'off they go into the bushes. Well, sir, you can imagine the Riggses' feelings when they'd fathomed this little piece of by-play, as you might call it. They put on the helmet of salvation, drew the sword of faith, and set about it hip and thigh, if you'll pardon the phrase, Sir. But it wasn't easy. To begin with, they didn't know a whole lot of the language, and in any case the language was a pretty limited one for their purpose. Now English, for instance is pretty rich in words for wickedness, and fine juicy words they are. But since these heathen didn't even know what they were doing was wicked, they hadn't, so to put it, got very far with the fire-and-brimstone parts of their dictionary. But Mr and Mrs Riggs did all they could with the words they had got, and where there just weren't any that were suitable, they taught their pagans to say them, as best they could, in English. In that way, after a few months, they were at last able to carry on a serious conversation. At least, it was serious on the Riggses' side, but Mr Riggs told me that he had grave doubts whether the islanders were ever serious except when they had flowers in their hair. Still, when Mr and Mrs Riggs suggested that they should be baptized, they all agreed, including the old man, and he liked it so much they had to baptize him six times over, not liking to offend a man in his position, as you can well understand, sir.

'Things had got that far, and you must admit it was a start, when a terrible thing happened. You're a married man, Mr Prince, so I can speak freely in front of you. Mr Riggs was quite fond of Mrs Riggs, and in the intervals of their labours, he sometimes did with Mrs Riggs what married couples have every right to do. Unfortunately, sir, they were observed. Some peeping-tom, looking through the holes in the grass walls of their hut, saw them in bed together.

'Then the fat was in the fire. The old man called them to his hut and gave them a wigging such as Mr Riggs hadn't had since he left school. He didn't understand all of it, but he gathered enough to know that the old man was shocked and disgusted with them both. What was more, he had a drum beat and everybody in the island came and they were just as shocked and disgusted as he was. You see, sir, they'd done something so awful that nobody on the island had ever heard of it being done before. They'd made love to each other without a flower in their hair.

'The ship arrived soon after and cast anchor. The old man tied Mr and Mrs Riggs together and put them in a canoe, and they were paddled out to the ship, all the islanders canoeing around them or swimming. Then they all climbed on the ship, the old man as well, and hauled poor Mr Riggs and Mrs Riggs up after them. The Captain wanted to know the meaning of such an outrage and then the most unholy clamour broke out. The heathens – and you can't really blame them when you come to think of it, in fact you might say they were quick learners – the heathen pointed at Mr and Mrs Riggs and said: "Har-lot!" "Whore!" "Pig!" "Dirty!" "Vile!" "Scarlet Woman!" and a lot more. The Captain, judging by appearances, thought it best to up anchor, so he sailed away, and, sir, as Mr Riggs explained to me, appearances were none the better when they faced the Society back home. As I said, sir, they ended up in the outer darkness, just as I was before I joined our community, in which, if I may say so, sir, since you're kind enough to ask my opinion, a little touch of ceremony will never come amiss. It's something deep in human nature, sir, when affairs of a nuptial nature are afoot, and it's not wise to ignore it, as Mr and Mrs Riggs, good souls that they are, found out to their cost.'

*

Prince told Bunt that he was most grateful for his admonition. He also made him Master of any Ceremonies that he could think up within the budgetary limits of five pounds, and provided that Prince was not called upon to say anything.

'I've already written my sermon, Bunt,' he said, 'and I shall have a hard enough job remembering that. Otherwise, you have *carte blanche*. Go and talk to Mrs Prince. She's much of your opinion in the matter, and she'll be a great help.'

Blushing again, but this time with pleasure, Bunt struggled into his jacket and went obediently to find Julia. Prince searched for his book among the confusion of flower-stalks, leaves and vases, and found it. But then he noticed the clock in the gallery, and saw that it was later than he had thought. He put the book in his pocket and, rather glumly, returned to his lodgings to do what he had decided was his duty.

The day before he had summoned the four Lampeter Brethren who were to be bridegrooms, and now he found them obediently waiting for him. They all sat round his landlady's table in her tiny, crowded parlour. Prince then informed them that he would have a question to ask them, and that meantime he would open the meeting – for such it was – with a reading from the Song of Songs.

Now Prince, whatever his failings, shared at least one trait with the great religious teachers of all ages. He often found his disciples, and especially his most devoted ones, unbearably irritating. It was so at this meeting. As he looked round at their rapt expressions, their obedient eyes, and their pronounced air of leaving everything to him and not lifting a finger themselves, he felt that his question, though an honourable one to ask, would be a waste of time. To prevent himself from growing brusque in their presence, he exaggerated his priestly air, and used his most orotund voice, meanwhile wishing that the Brethren had been women, for women had a right to be helpless, and were, indeed, rather fetching at it.

He finished the Song of Solomon, altered the stops a little in his vocal console, and said:

'Brother Thomas, Brother Lewis, Brother William, and Brother William Cobbe, we are gathered here together today in the light of the new revelation. May our deliberations be blessed.'

'Amen,' said George Thomas, in the light, clipped inflexion he had picked up in France.

'Amen,' said Lewis Price, with a beautiful expression on his handsome face, imitating, but not very well, Prince's rich voice.

'Amen,' said William Puddy, hushed with admiration as he stared at Price's bowed head.

'Amen,' said Cobbe, the loudest of all, sending his voice resounding through the imaginary chapel of the imaginary monastery in which he spent most of his time.

'Now,' said Prince, 'that we are on the threshold of the first engage ... that is,' he corrected himself, 'the first betrothal in our community, it is my duty to ask you, each of you, if you wish to withdraw.'

'No!'

'No!'

'No!'

'No!' they said in turn, as Prince knew quite well they would. He tried again:

'As your spiritual leader ever since the days when we first went down on our knees together and asked for heaven's guidance in our lives, I must ask you all to consider your answer carefully.' In spite of himself, Prince could not prevent giving a schoolmasterly edge to the last word. 'In consenting to become the husbands, albeit the spiritual ones, of these four women, you will be aware that the world will consider you their carnal husbands as well. Among us, who are enlightened, the distinction has no meaning ...' and at this point Lewis Price nodded his handsome head vigorously, '... but to those still in the outer darkness,' Prince went on, and did not fail to observe that he was borrowing some of his rhetoric from Bunt, 'you will be contracting a marriage such as any other man may make, with the duties and obligations that attend such things.'

All four murmured their agreement, as easily, Prince felt, as though they were confirming the date.

'Your betrothals will have far-reaching consequences,' said Prince, throwing all the earnestness of which he was capable into his manner, in an attempt to penetrate their loyal devotion.

'Of course they will,' said William Puddy, with a smile which radiated faith, 'but we know that you have foreseen them all.'

'The joyful sense that our revelation has brought to us must not make us . . .' Prince trembled perilously on the verge of the word 'smug', but recovered himself, '. . . insensible to wordly considerations, however much we may have the inner certainty that we shall, in the assurance of our election by Providence, transcend them easily. For instance,' he went on, 'this betrothal will, there can be no doubt, be frowned upon by those officials of the old dispensation such as the rectors some of you have hitherto served, and by those pillars of self-righteousness, your bishops. Have you considered that?'

'Oh, *bishops!*' said Lewis Price, laughing. 'Yes, the bishops have frowned all right. They've frowned so hard they'll have permanent furrows, I fear. Brother George's bishop and *our* bishop', he said, indicating himself and Puddy, 'sent us letters as soon as we came here, telling us to return. As a matter of fact,' he said, 'since we haven't done so, I believe we have lost our jobs.' The other two curates nodded in cheerful agreement. 'But we don't take much notice of their Lordships nowadays. *You're* our bishop, now.'

'Yes,' said Prince, and felt a twinge of sympathy with the episcopacy. 'Then, as your bishop, I must ask you if you have considered the question of money.'

'Ah, money,' said Brother George, with a knowing look. 'Ah, yes. Money.' He shook his head, sagely, but as usual, said nothing more.

'It is a sign of the approval from on high,' said Prince, 'that our little community has, in recent weeks, received generous offerings from those who have heard our message. We have been able to maintain our hall, and to pay those who have been giving you, my beloved disciples, shelter and food. But I must tell you that we cannot, we must not, hope that this sign from above will necessarily continue.' He paused. Not even these men in front of him, he thought, could be so simple as not to see what he was driving at.

'I've a little of my own,' said Brother George. 'About three hundred a year. I didn't know you were paying for the lodging. I thought the landlady was a believer.'

'As for me,' said Lewis Price, 'I've got about a hundred a year, as it is. More to come, I hope, as uncles and aunts drop off. But not much.'

'I'm rich,' said young William Puddy. 'Or at least I was. But since I insisted on attending your meetings, sir, my father's cut me off with a shilling.'

'*What?*' said Prince, sharply.

'I have some savings from my post with the railway,' said Cobbe. 'Two, three hundred maybe. I'm not sure. I've been dipping into it. But, of course, the whole lot is yours for the asking. A community like ours has no use for personal property. When we are finally established, all, every penny must be in common.'

'Oh yes, yes,' the three other brethren agreed, and Prince noticed that young Puddy agreed as heartily as any.

'And,' said Brother George, 'I suppose the young ladies . . I mean . . . er . . . Sister Harriet, and Agnes and Clara and Louisa will feel much the same way? I hope so; oh, yes, indeed, I hope so,' he said. 'They must be strong in faith like us.'

'I hope so, too,' said Prince. 'But they are women, brothers, and they depend upon their father for all that they have and all that they may have in the future. Their father, in spite of the freewill offering which he made us on a generous scale, is a sick man, and sick men . . .'

He saw the too readily understanding expressions with which

his warnings were being received, and his command over his language finally ebbed. 'Well, brothers,' he finished, 'there's many a slip between the cup and the lip.'

They said nothing. They continued to gaze at him devotedly. He sighed. 'I want you to remember', he said, wearily, 'that I said so. That is all.' He picked up his book and pushed back his chair.

Brother George coughed and said: 'I wonder if I might say a few words, Brother Henry, on this occasion?' Without waiting for an answer, he went on: 'I feel that we would all like to tell you of the sense, the wonderful sense, of spiritual well-being, of joyous illumination, of understanding which these last few days have brought to us.' Appreciative murmurs from the other three warned Prince that they, too, in due course, would have their say. He pulled his chair back to the table, leaned his forehead on his hand and listened, while one after the other, they exercised the privilege of all true disciples, which is to repeat to their master what he has already told them, but told them better. As their fervent voices filled the tiny room, Prince reflected that there was now nobody at all who spoke to him as a human being, except Julia, who left unsaid most things that she cared deeply about, and Bunt. He thought fondly of Bunt during the next, interminable, half-hour.

*

When he went across the road that evening to the meeting, Bunt, respectfully, took charge of him. Prince was unable to get past the entrance foyer, so great was the crowd, and Bunt, taking his elbow, steered him into a small room near the platform used by speakers while awaiting their entrance. Here he said:

'They're flocking like bees to a jam-pot, sir, and I think we'll have difficulty getting them all seated. Would you mind very much, sir, if Mrs Prince played a little music on the harmonium?'

At this very moment the harmonium began.

'I've no objection, Bunt,' said Prince.

'Ah,' said Bunt, dabbing his perspiring forehead. 'I thought you wouldn't have, sir. Well, sir, there's another thing I've got to ask you ... wait a bit, sir, I ...' He searched in his pockets and brought out a crumpled envelope on which he had pencilled, in a large looping handwriting, the order of the proceedings.

'Yes, sir, here it is. If instead of going straight on to the platform as you usually do, you would hold back a little till I give the signal, if you'll excuse the presumption, sir ...'

'Sergeant Bunt,' said Prince, 'I will do anything you say except kiss ...' He was stopped short by Bunt's look of alarm.

'Please, sir,' said Bunt, 'please don't say you won't kiss the ladies, sir.'

'Except', Prince finished his sentence reassuringly, 'kiss Brothers George, William, Lewis and William. I have no objection to kissing the ladies, Bunt.'

'Ah,' said Bunt, relieved, 'I thought you wouldn't. Now, if you'll excuse me, sir,' and he bustled off, worried, but happy.

When Prince, at a militarily precise signal from Bunt, walked on to the platform, the audience, following the lead of some well-drilled woman in the forward seats, rose silently, and stood till Prince himself sat down. Prince placed his notes on the table in front of him and was about to get up and launch upon the incantatory beginning of his address, when he caught Julia's eye. Following her glance he saw a piece of paper under the water bottle on which were scrawled the words: '*Wait pl for happy cuppels to come in*', and obedient to Bunt's written orders, he waited. Julia played the harmonium softly, and Prince examined the hall.

The seats on the ground floor were full, the gallery was full, with people standing several deep at the back, and along each side wall was a row of men who had given up their seats to women. The chairs in the front row of the hall had been taken away. In their place, surrounded by banks of flowers were eight gilt armchairs, upholstered in slightly worn red plush.

These, Prince learned later, had been obtained by Bunt from the local theatre. The touring company, having decided not to play that night because of the fewness of the bookings, had sportingly agreed to lend some of its box seats to the rival attraction.

Julia now played some triumphant chords on the harmonium, Bunt flung open the doors at the back of the hall, and to murmurs of admiration, the four couples, each of the women with a white gloved hand laid on the arm of her escort, came processionally down the middle aisle. Prince covertly showed his astonishment to Julia, who looked very pleased; for she had spent the afternoon helping to dress the Nottidge sisters in the utmost splendour that their wardrobe would permit. Now, with the brethren's hair shining as brightly as the brethren's shoes, the Nottidge jewellery gleaming in the lamplight, the fine silks of the women's voluminous dresses, and the music, the eight lovers made a telling picture. They seated themselves in the red plush chairs, the men bowing, and the women with a swirl of skirts that did Bunt's heart good to see.

When Prince's sermon was over and he had kissed each of the sisters tenderly upon the lips, the meeting came to its formal end. But the lovers had to make their way through a barrier of outstretched hands, and some women of the audience, unable to get near them, moved by this first betrothal in a sinless dispensation, stood on chairs and blew them kisses.

'Look,' said Julia to Prince. 'Bunt's got tears rolling down his cheeks. What will he do when we have the wedding, I wonder?'

'He will be much less moved,' said Prince. 'He will be fighting down the old Adam.'

'Anyway,' said Julia. 'It has all been a great success. The collection should be very large. By the way,' she said, turning to her husband, 'I saw Josiah today. He looks very weak. I hope,' she said, ambiguously, 'that everything will be all right.'

*

In the small hours of that night, Josiah Nottidge went to find the truth concerning all those questions that Prince had so glibly answered in his sermons. Harriet was with him when he died. She told her sisters that he laughed a little and then closed his eyes. But there she did not tell the truth. Josiah had laughed, but then he had fought long and bitterly for his life, as dying men must do, and especially Josiah, who had found so much in life to entertain him. But he did not live to see the strangest comedy of all that his money produced, unless, perhaps the Abode of Love was haunted by his happy ghost.

*

Nottidge was buried in Brighton. Since he had never set foot inside his parish church in Bermondsey, Prince saw no point in burying his body there – and it was Prince to whom all the sisters turned in their affliction. It was Prince who summoned Josiah's relatives, a grey, timid group, quite dazzled by the worldliness of Brighton, and unnerved by the phalanx of clergymen, who seemed to have taken charge of everything from Josiah's corpse to his bereaved daughters. It was Prince who, in a masterly fashion, solved the problem of letting Cornelia know in time for her to come to the funeral from faraway Ireland. He remembered Larkspur, and sent him a note, posthaste, inviting his help. Larkspur, delighted to display his modernity, made use of the still novel telegraph to send a telegram (or as some more correctly called it, a telegrapheme) to Bristol. The packet boat took it to Ireland, the post-chaise took it to Cornelia, who had time to weep, to be consoled, and to arrive, with her husband, on the day of the funeral, by first-class reserved carriages, on each one of which Larkspur had tied a large mourning bow of black silk.

In a word, the funeral was a great success, for all save Cornelia. In the first place she had come prepared to fling herself across her father's bier, and heart-brokenly beg his pardon for running away. She found it quite impossible to do anything of the sort; the schedule of arrangements expertly followed by no less than four clergymen allowed her scarcely a minute in which to look upon her dear father's face, before he was screwed down. Secondly, her broad-shouldered husband did not cut the figure that she had hoped he would. A horse-breeder can never look as much at home at a funeral as clergymen, and her sisters' fiancees carried all before them. Cornelia's husband, being large, got frequently in the way, and being among total strangers at the obsequies of a man he had never seen, he went to great trouble to look sorrowful. The result was that he moved about with an expression of such ferocious gloom that it seemed that the dead man must have done him some mortal injury and death had cheated him of revenge. Brother George and his companions, on the other hand, were sorrowful to a nicety. Cornelia told herself that they would not look so much at ease if they were on horseback, but it was not much consolation. She hoped, desperately, that her husband would not examine the matched pairs of jet horses that drew the hearse, but, as she observed through the Venetian blinds, he did. He had slipped out for a few minutes in order to look at them, and the coachman had to draw his attention to the fact that the procession was about to come out of the house. He stood, large and embarrassed, by the railing, until he could slip in among the mourners.

That day, Cornelia resigned herself to the fact that her marriage, though romantic, would always lack *éclat*. She was tender to her sisters, gave them her blessings, and after the will was read, went quietly home to Ireland where she stayed, with but rare visits to England, for the rest of her life.

*

While Josiah's lawyer was reading Josiah's testament, Prince stayed in his lodgings with Julia. They sat in their landlady's narrow parlour, Prince pretending to read and Julia pretending to sew.

When the front door bell rang briskly, they both got to their feet, both made for the hallway, and both sat sheepishly down again as their landlady hurried to greet her visitor.

He came, a moment later, into the parlour, a tall, thin man with close-cropped white hair, a large, inquisitive nose, and a black leather bag under his arm. He announced himself as Josiah's lawyer, shook hands, and sat at the table.

'A sad business,' he said, and shook his head several times.

Prince, his mouth dry, agreed that it was.

'Prime of life,' said the lawyer. 'Snatched away.' He opened his bag and took out some papers. He whistled a little tune under his breath, as he deliberately and slowly shuffled his documents.

The door opened. Prince, already unnerved by the whistling, jumped. It was the landlady.

'Would you like some sherry to offer the gentleman?' she said, scarcely raising her voice. 'I've brought it in case you did.'

'Ah,' said the lawyer, with a loud sniff, 'sherry. Splendid!' He returned to sorting his papers, and his nearly inaudible whistling. While the sherry was being poured and handed round, Prince, in an effort to control himself, tried hard to make out the lawyer's tune. He had just discovered that it was a galloping version of one of the hymns they had sung at the funeral, when the lawyer said, with an explosive sniff:

'Your health, madam. Your health, sir. A sad business. Snatched away, in the prime of life, leaving five orphans.' He downed the sherry, smacked his lips, sniffed enormously and said:

'Now, sir, down to our muttons. I'll not keep you waiting. We're men of the world, sir, and we understand each other's feelings on occasions like this. Nobody wants to be disrespectful to the late departed, but nobody wants to be kept *hanging around*.' He leaned his great nose confidentially towards them, drew in an enormous quantity of air, leaned once more back in his chair, and whistled under his breath.

This time, Prince noticed the tune was 'God Save the Queen'.

'I imagine,' said Prince, with deliberation, 'that one at least of the orphaned ladies will have no fear for the future. Mr Nottidge was kind enough to show me his will before he died and ...'

The lawyer stopped whistling. His pursed-up lips relaxed slowly into a broad smile. '*That* will,' he said, and shook his head. 'Such a sense of humour, the late departed, such a sense of humour.' He laughed, as silently as he whistled.

'There was another will?' asked Prince.

The lawyer nodded, unable to speak for his silent laughter. He controlled himself, wiped his eyes and said: 'Not that I approved. "Destroy it, Mr Nottidge," I said, when he made another, "destroy it," but he wouldn't. "I'll have some fun with this," he said. And so he did, so he did. Showed it around, swearing he'd never alter a word of *"that parchment"*, didn't he?'

'Yes.'

'So he told me. Well, he didn't. Not of *"that parchment"*. You see?'

'I see.'

'Not of *that parchment*, Mrs Prince,' he said, turning to Julia to make sure that she understood the joke. 'Do you follow, Mrs Prince? Priceless, wasn't it? Priceless.' The smile faded from his face suddenly. 'Now, to business, if you'll pardon me. I understand that you are head, Mr Prince, of a religious organization which ...' he consulted his papers, '... ah ... um ... which holds that we must all be prepared at any moment for the Apocalypse.'

'I am. We do.'

'Well, what of it?'

'I beg your pardon?'

'What of it, I say,' said the lawyer, with sudden animation. 'I've thought it over and I say, "what of it?". Let them drag us through every court in the land. Let 'em take it to the House of Lords and then what'll they find? They'll find the Archbishop of Canterbury saying the same thing. They can't get us there, that's certain. But what about this?' He stubbed his forefinger on a paper in front of him. 'You say the members of your sect will never die. Is that so?'

'Yes.'

The lawyer sniffed. He whistled a windy stave or two.

'That's bad.' The lawyer shook his head gloomily.

'I thought,' said Prince, sharply, 'that it was one of the better parts of my teaching. And we do not, by the way, refer to our community as a sect.'

'Henry,' warned Julia, as she saw his temper rising, but the lawyer had raised his finger, and with one eye screwed up, was regarding intently an imaginary trial taking place on the other side of the room. 'Suppose,' he said, wagging his finger, 'somebody does die. And they prove it. Exhibit A. Death Certificate. They hand it to the Clerk of the Court.' He dramatically imitated the dialogue of the visionary trial. ' "Death Certificate, eh?" "Yes, me lud." "Well, Mr Prince?" – that's to you in the box. "What have you got to say to that?" ' He leaned forward like a bullying counsel. ' "What have you got to say to *that*, Mr Prince." ' He leaned back in his chair. He sniffed. 'Fixed. That's what we are.'

'My promise is that those who have faith will never die,' said Prince.

The lawyer swung his nose at Prince; he beat the table with the flat of his hand. 'It is, is it?' he said, delightedly. He turned swiftly to his court scene. 'So up our man rises and says: "But the disciple in question, me lud, did not have faith. He did not have faith, me lud, and that is why, according to us, he died. The terms of my client's promise were not infringed." ' The lawyer banged on the table. ' "Case dismissed." '

'You expect that there will be a case?' asked Julia.

'I'm a lawyer, ma'am, and it's my professional duty to expect a case where there's a large sum of money involved. But have no fear. You've as much right to that thirty thousand pounds as Josiah Nottidge had himself.

'Thirty . . .' said Prince, and lost his voice.

'Thirty thousand to begin with. The young ladies have got six thousand each. Four sixes are twenty-four. Right? Unless I am mistaken. Correct me if I am wrong.'

Julia and Prince nodded in unison.

'They inform me that they wish to use this to contribute – buy shares in – put it how you will – they want to make it over to your organization. If they marry – well, well, I'll explain that later. Now, sir: Miss Harriet gets the rest of the property and says she wants to make good Cornelia's share, that young lady not wishing, so I understand, to contribute, being already married outside the fold. Five sixes are thirty. Right? Good. Then there's Miss Harriet's own fortune, which will come along in dribs and drabs, as we get the thing straightened out. There's a hundred thousand there, if there's a penny.'

'Will you,' said Julia, a little hoarsely, 'have some more sherry?'

'Thank you, ma'am, I will,' he said eyeing them both keenly; and when Henry, his hand shaking uncontrollably, spilled the sherry on the table, the lawyer, with his first, open, loud laugh, said: 'Steady, boys, steady, we'll fight and we'll conquer again and again, eh, Mr Prince?' With that he whistled forcibly but still under his breath, the whole of the rest of 'Hearts of Oak' without annoying Prince at all.

He gave Prince the details of the will; he assured Prince that if the sisters married, as was planned, they fully intended to make their portions over to their husbands, with the knowledge that they would go into the fund; he confirmed that there was nothing in the law to stop them doing so; and finally, he offered his services to the new church. Then he left.

The landlady saw him out. Then, as anxious as anyone as to the outcome of the meeting, she ventured to put her head in at the parlour door. She saw Prince with Julia in his arms, and both of them revolving in a sort of confined but expressive dance in the narrow space between the table and the wall. She retired, satisfied that everything must be well, as indeed it was.

7

An English Harem

HENRY JAMES PRINCE now did two noble actions; they were the only noble actions of his life, but there were two of them, and it is not given to many of us to do two fine things.

The first was that he gave up preaching. He had a fine voice, a handsome presence and a devoted following; yet he appeared on a platform only once more in his life, and that was to announce that he would never mount one again because he had nothing more to say. It is a shining example to everyone with a fine voice, a handsome manner and nothing more to say, and it is a pity that it is not more widely followed. It is no doubt a difficult act; saints who have inflicted upon themselves the most searching austerities, have not been able to rise to the final austerity of holding their tongues. But Prince was not a saint and it may have been a little easier for him. He had a gift for coolly observing himself in action (a gift which is disastrous to saints) and it is clear that what he observed of himself on a platform he did not like. So he stepped down, forever.

It will be seen that Prince had many faults, but he was not wholly a charlatan – not, at least, when he had enough money to do as he pleased with his life. Perhaps he had been something of a charlatan when he had been poor: when one is poor, one is many undesirable things. He needed money to bring out the finer points of his character, like the rest of us, including, we may note, St Francis of Assisi, who, when he took his great decision to purify his faith, was a rich young man.

The second of Prince's noble acts was to decide to take his money and his followers, not to the metropolis, where he would have notoriety and perhaps fame; not to some part of the country in which nobody knew him, and where he could find peace, but to Charlinch, the village whose inhabitants had driven him out of his first cure of souls. Like many acts of courage, it was a success. The farmers of Charlinch who had driven out the penniless curate, welcomed the returning spiritual leader with thirty thousand pounds in his pocket.

*

The exodus from Brighton to Charlinch was an extraordinary affair. Prince was aware that the audiences he had gathered at the meeting-hall in Brighton contained both sheep and goats. He also knew that the rumour that he had come into money would attract more followers, and those mainly goats. His task was to separate the two.

He did this by abruptly closing the meeting-hall. He then let it be known that he was going to Weymouth, another watering place along the coast, but nearer Charlinch, of which Promised Land he as yet made no mention. All who wished to follow him could do so; but they must follow forthwith. He thereupon set out, in a procession of carriages, with Julia, the Nottidge sisters, and their four betrothed. He also let it be known that at Weymouth he would make the final, and most important part of the Great Declaration. Finally, he engaged outriders and postillions, who wore a uniform livery, not yet that of Prince's own household – there was no time to design one – but still the most magnificent that could be hired in the Old Steyn, the centre of fashionable Brighton.

His departure from his lodgings was therefore a tremendous affair with horses stamping, coachmen cracking their whips, postillions bawling, and outriders creating as much confusion in the narrow streets as their generous fees called for. To add to the spectacle, scores of fine ladies, surprised and dismayed, gathered on the kerbstone and wept. Many of them tried to speak with Prince to persuade him to stay. He took notice neither of their words nor their tears. He impassively supervised the departure, handed Julia into the carriage, waited until the betrothed couples had settled themselves in their own vehicles, and then, lifting a finger, gave the order to go. His whole bearing told the onlookers that the remedy for their grief was simple. They could pack their traps and follow him.

The one person, besides the sisters and the four brethren, who was exempted from this intense spiritual pressure was Sergeant Bunt. Prince had consulted him closely in the whole matter. Bunt had suggested the postillions and outriders; he had recruited them from among his waterfront friends; he had hired their uniforms and he had bribed them to kick up as much fuss and pother as they could. He then had taken the post-chaise to Weymouth. When the cavalcade, two days later, pulled up at the Royal Hotel, he was there, resplendent in the uniform of a major-domo, standing on the steps bareheaded, and already surrounded by a gaping crowd of some three hundred persons.

*

It was altogether a great day for Bunt. Prince's party, after they had rested a while from their journey, came downstairs and gathered in the ornate ballroom, made even more grandiose by the florist's baskets of lilies which Bunt had placed in various striking groups. All present shook hands with an awed notary public, also recruited by Bunt, and Prince, without further ado, went into a form of marriage service, devised by himself, but held in deference to Bunt's strong feeling that there should be some such ceremony.

There were, officially, no witnesses to this marriage except the notary public and Julia. But Matthew Bunt had omitted to close the great folding doors, and the corridor outside was so crammed with sightseers that they edged, imperceptibly, on to the ballroom floor.

When the ceremony was done, the brides kissed – there were no rings – and the bridegrooms congratulated; the brides, one by one, made a simple declaration to the notary public that they willingly gave their property to their husbands whom they accepted as husbands according to the law. The Brethren, now married men, followed with an equally simple declaration that, according to the tenets of their faith, they placed all their possessions in the hands of their spiritual leader, Henry James Prince.

When the notary public had accepted the post twenty years before, he had never in his wildest imaginings thought that he would have to take public note of such extraordinary proceedings, and could do little now but gaze in astonishment from face to face, nod his head, and pretend to write things down. He was led off, finally, by Bunt, who called for biscuits and a bottle of the hotel's best wine, which he put on a table beside the notary, shook him heartily by the hand, and left him. This completed the notary's ruin and when, later, Josiah Nottidge's lawyer called for his documents to complete the legal transfer of the money, the lawyer, sniffing disdainfully with his large nose, found that he had to draw up the papers himself. But, in due course, the thing was done, and by the end of the week Prince was legally a rich man.

Meantime, the faithful had been coming in daily from Brighton, and even from Stoke, the scene of Prince's second curacy. They were all told of what had happened concerning the money, and they were all told that, should they wish to follow Prince further, they must do likewise. Those who wished to live with Prince in the new community must give up all they had. Those who wished only to be numbered among the saved could make a gift of only one part. Those – and there was a tight-fisted minority – who did not wish to give anything at all, or who said they might, later, or who said they would like to think it over, were kindly told to go away. Those – and this included Mrs Cusack, the caretaker of the hall – who had nothing to give at all, were lodged in the town and told that Prince would have need of them, in due course. They had only to promise to serve him, which they willingly did.

The comings and goings, the bustle, the gossip, the rumours and the general air of excitement were such as the little town had never before witnessed: and when Prince announced that he would bring the Great Declaration to an end on Thursday evening, in the ballroom at eight o'clock precisely, Bunt had hastily to add to the notice that admission would be by invitation only. Cards were engraved with a space for the name of the fortunate follower, and these were given to Bunt to deliver. He did so, but with great deliberation.

First he issued them to the disciples who had already decided to give all they had to the common fund. Then, for a whole day, he issued no more. This mild turn of the rack produced a number of devotees who discovered with joy that their business affairs were simpler than they had expected, and they were willing and ready to give their all. When they had done so, they got their cards. Another day passed, with no cards issued, and a further group of disciples, particularly those who were making only a contribution, decided to make bigger ones. When they had done so, they, too, got their cards. By Thursday at seven-thirty p.m., two hundred people had been gathered into the fold, and Prince declared that he would take no more. The doors of the ballroom were, this time, very firmly closed, and two hundred saved souls, excited, but also relieved, rose to their feet as Prince mounted the platform for the last time.

*

Harriet, Clara and Louisa were among his most contented listeners. For a week they had been sampling the delights of marriage and they had found that Cornelia had spoken no less than the truth. Their husbands had been gallant beyond their expectations, and, for full measure, pressed down and flowing over, they could reflect that they were also married, in a sense, to the handsome man on the platform.

Agnes looked less happy.

She had faced the prospect of her bridal night with some misgiving. She wondered whether her habitual shyness would undo her. In the event, she found the whole thing much easier than she had expected, or indeed, could have wished. No sooner had they retired to their bridal suite than 'Mossoo' tactfully pointed to a camp-bed in the dressing-room and said:

'Well, Agnes, my dear, I shall sleep there. Good night, my dear,' and he kissed her hair and left her. He was about to shut the door when Agnes said:

'Oh, George . . . George . . . don't shut the door, George.'

'No?' said George. 'Very well. But I thought you would prefer it so.'

'Not really,' said Agnes. 'You see ... you see,' she said, with a stroke of inspiration, 'I'm afraid of sleeping alone. I've always slept with my sisters, and – '

'Of course, I quite understand,' sai dGeorge. 'There. I've put my boot against the door, so now you can be quite sure it won't slam to. I usually read a little; I hope my light won't keep you awake.'

'No,' said Agnes, doubtfully..'I don't think so.'

George undressed and went to bed, but out of sight. Agnes did the same. She got into bed and drew the clothes to her chin. She stared at the ceiling with bewildered eyes. She was not, of course, innocent of the meaning of marriage. She had been brought up with four sisters, one of them no better than she should be, and she had acquired a considerable fund of know-ledge from them. But it was all theoretical, in the nature of things, and poor Agnes felt that the bases of her knowledge were crumbling.

'George,' she said at last, 'are you still reading?'

'Yes, my dear.'

'George, is marriage always like this?'

'By no means, Agnes. I would not like to tell you what it is like. Indeed, I can scarcely claim to know. I have never felt the slightest interest in such things. That is why I welcome our spiritual union so warmly.'

'Yes,' said Agnes. 'But isn't the spiritual the same thing as the carnal? I mean, like Mr Prince says.'

'A better way of putting it is that the carnal is spiritual – with us, that is, the enlightened ones.'

Agnes did not feel, at that moment, enlightened. She lay silent, struggling with her thoughts.

'Although, of course,' said her invisible husband, 'you *could* say that the *spiritual* is carnal, with us. It's a fine point.'

'Yes, isn't it,' said Agnes, her hopes fluttering.

'It sounds as though it amounts to the same thing. But I don't think that that is the meaning of Prince's teaching,' said her husband. 'Putting it round that way is just a quibble.'

'A quibble,' said Agnes, mournfully. 'Just a quibble. I see.'

'I don't mean that *you're* quibbling, my dear,' said George, gallantly.

'Thank you,' said Agnes. 'I wouldn't like you to think I was the sort of woman who quibbled,' she said. She sounded so sad that George's conscience struck him.

'I'm really being very selfish,' he said.

'Yes,' said Agnes.

'You have had an exciting and tiring day. I won't read a line more; I shall put out the light straight away.'

He was as good as his word. Privately he determined to ask Prince in the morning if it was absolutely necessary to share rooms with his spiritual wife. He supposed, going to sleep, that it must be symbolical, but it would be inconvenient, he felt, if it went on too long.

*

Thus when Prince intoned his customary opening, 'Sin must be pardoned in the mind ere it is subdued in the heart,' Agnes sadly reflected that she was farther off than ever from understanding what he meant. She supposed her more fortunate sisters must know better. She glanced at them and imagined them to be busy forgiving the most elaborate and mysterious sins in their minds, while they subdued others, committed on previous occasions and no less veiled from Agnes's knowledge, in their experienced hearts.

But a change in Prince's voice, and sudden stillness in the audience, brought her back to what was being said, and that, when she grasped it, was sufficiently remarkable to make her temporarily forget her troubles.

Prince was no longer using the luscious vocabulary of the Song of Songs. He had gone back to his other favourite, the Book of the Revelation, and he was speaking of the Apocalypse. It was coming, he said. It was coming in the lifetime of those who were listening to him. It would be a terrible affair – he quoted a few passages – but he seemed casual, almost bored, with it. He unfolded the reason for his calm. He had to inform them that the Last Judgement had already taken place, quietly, like the passing over of the Angel of Death. It had been vouchsafed to him in his vision that he had been saved, and so had those – those, but no others – who were in that room with him that very night.

The rest of his speech was an anti-climax, as he fully intended. Nothing could be more relaxing than to know one was irrevocably saved, and he aimed to create an atmosphere of complete ease. His nonchalance was perhaps the most convincing argument of the evening, and his nonchalance spread. His listeners coughed, shuffled their feet, and eased their limbs. Smiles were exchanged between saved friends. Bunt stepped out of the hall and made an inviting clatter among the plates of refreshments that were arranged outside.

Meanwhile Prince explained what the saved should do. They had to wait for the Apocalypse. Prince had decided that this could best be done in a quiet community of saved souls living in harmony and love in the country.

At this point he grew reminiscent. Looking back into his own past, as though peering through a telescope at the incomprehensible antics of some distant figures, he recalled that at Charlinch he had met with misunderstanding and hostility. Two of his brethren – they were in the hall at this moment – had gallantly purchased a piece of land and built a chapel, or meeting-house, or conventicle (the name of such places no longer mattered) in which he could carry on his mission. He had never used it. But now, he had bought the land on which it stood; he had bought, moreover, an adjacent mansion, its outhouses, and the meadows around it. Here, at Spaxton, near Charlinch, would be their waiting-place, where they could live peaceably until the heavens rolled up like a scroll and angels conducted them to their heavenly thrones. The place would be called the Agapemone, or, as he quickly translated for the benefit of the less scholarly, THE ABODE OF LOVE. He fixed a date, not far ahead, when all the saved should gather under its roof, there to remain for ever, which would not, of course, be a very long time.

*

Spaxton itself was very beautiful. It was a valley bottom, remote from the world; the nearest town was four miles away over a poor road. The soil in the valley was fat; the hills were clothed with trees. Streams and rills abounded, and they rarely froze because the harshest winds of winter never found their way into the fortunate valley.

There was a large house next to the unfinished church, with some stables, outhouses and some cottages. Here, in the first place, the faithful lived, the favourite disciples in the house with Prince, the less favoured in the cottages, which were allocated strictly in accordance with the money that each person had contributed to the common fund. But there was by no means room for all who wished to come, and Prince immediately began to build.

He called in masons, bricklayers, carpenters, plumbers, gardeners, foresters, ditchers, and labourers of every description. He proceeded to make himself a large country seat. There is nothing like building to make a man popular in a community. Building operations look – and are – expensive. Although a great number of people, from kings downwards, have started buildings and not had enough money to finish them, nobody seems to remember the fact when a new work begins. Prince knew this, and he built on a lavish scale. Prince knew, besides, that every labourer and craftsman whom he engaged became one of his supporters in the surrounding countryside.

He built wisely and well, throwing out an orderly complex of wings, courtyards and dependencies, preserving some of the cottages, destroying others, building porticoes, walks and terraces, until there was not only room for all who wished to live with him but, even more importantly, space enough in which to avoid them if he wanted.

Prince also completed the church that had once been built for him. In the building of the Abode he had been as sensible and sound as a burgher merchant who had recently bought himself a title and was constructing a country seat for himself and his descendants. In the matter of the church, however, his theological training once more led him into peculiarity.

He refused to finish the tower. He had no use for it, he said, since towers are for bells, bells are for calling Christians to the church service, and there were going to be no services at all. There was no need for them; in Prince's view, they would be something of a swindle. It was no use coming to church and praying to be saved, if you were damned: and it was as little use praying to be saved if you were *not* damned: that is, if you had formed part of the shining company in the ballroom of the Royal Hotel, Weymouth.

But as many people had noticed before him, a church, if warmed, is a fine and commodious place. Prince therefore furnished the church in the most solid and comfortable taste, installing the fireplace, the carpet and the palms in pots that we saw at the beginning of this story. As for the billiard table, that, like many of the strange things that people do, had the simplest and most human explanation.

One day, when he and Sergeant Bunt had been working together, supervising the workmen who were repointing the church walls, Prince said to Bunt:

'Sergeant Bunt, when I think of all the things I owe to your sagacity and good advice, I feel that I would like to make you a present. Sergeant Bunt, what, next to the ladies, is the thing which most takes your fancy?'

Sergeant Bunt blushed, brushed the lime dust from his hands, blushed even more deeply, and at last said:

'Billiards, if you'll excuse the remark, sir.'

A billiard table and its appurtenances was delivered to Spaxton from Bristol before the week was out.

＊

The Abode of Love was not properly finished for two years. By that time it sheltered, in all, and including numerous domestic servants, some forty saved souls. But the centre of the community was the main house, next the church, with its two wings. Here Prince lived, with his favoured disciples, who were Julia, the Lampeter Brethren who had married the Signs, and the four sisters themselves. Life in this heart of the community was, at this stage, very tranquil. One day was very like another, as befitted people who were spending their time in waiting for the Day of Days.

The morning began early, at five o'clock. A maidservant (she had worked in Prince's Brighton lodgings and had follo·ved him) cleaned the fireplaces, lit the fires and then woke the butler with a cup of strong tea, an English habit, then and now, but in those days usually confined to the working classes. The butler had been a waiter in Weymouth and had invested his life's savings in Prince to the great advantage, as it turned out, of his immortal soul and his status below stairs. He now dressed and went to wake Sergeant Bunt, also with a cup of strong tea, in which on cold mornings he stirred a little whisky.

Sergeant Bunt now rose and dressed himself in his majordomo's uniform. Once attired, he made the rounds of the house, carefully inspecting every detail. This was a most impressive ritual and it held the rest of the staff in terror, as well it might, for in posture, expression, language and if necessary, roaring, Bunt based himself meticulously upon Captain Overton. The inspection usually ended in the vast underground kitchen.

Here Mrs Cusack, no longer a caretaker but a housekeeper, presided over a throng of lesser servants, all saved, and all being paid excellent wages out of the common fund. A great boiler would be steaming with water for the Brothers' and Sisters' morning baths, while Mrs Cusack kept a watchful eye on the bell indicator.

So far nothing differed in the routine of the Abode from the morning observances of any large, well-to-do household of the time. The indicator, however, was unique. The top row of holes, in which, when the bell was rung, a red disk quivered, were labelled 'Brother George', 'Brother Lewis', 'Brother William', 'Brother William (C)' and, at the end, 'The Beloved', the name by which Prince was known in the community. The bottom row, which connected with another series of rooms was labelled 'Sister Julia', 'Sister Harriet', 'Sister Agnes', 'Sister Clara', and 'Sister Louisa'.

It will be seen at once that 'Mossoo' had won his point. Brothers and Sisters, married though they might be, lived in separate wings. But this arrangement was not, of course, inflexible, except in the case of 'Mossoo'. Generally speaking, the red disk would flutter in the hole once, briefly. Then the chambermaids would be sent scurrying by Mrs Cusack, a copper jug would be dipped in the boiler, steaming hot water procured, and carried upstairs with clean towels and other paraphernalia.

But occasionally the red disk would quiver repeatedly in the hole, and the warning bell would jangle three times. When that happened two copper jugs would be dipped in the boiler, two sets of towels piled on the chambermaid's arm, and she would hurry upstairs to the room where a Brother, having crossed the night before from one wing to the other, had carnally-spiritually or spiritually-carnally spent the intervening hours with his wife.

The Beloved's bell was usually the last to ring, because he was a late riser. This invariably rang once only, but it was equally the rule to take two jugs of hot water. This was done by the senior-most chambermaid, who knocked respectfully on the door, and said: 'Good morning, Beloved.' On being invited to enter, she would go in, deposit the cans by the washstand and return to draw aside the curtains. She would then report on the weather. 'A fine day, sir', or 'Rainy, I'm afraid, sir', or 'There's a nip in the air, sir'. Servants used Prince's title of Beloved only when saying good morning or good night. For the rest of the day, he was addressed as 'sir' like any ordinary mortal.

When the daylight had illuminated the room sufficiently to see the bed, the senior chambermaid would then, and not till then, say 'Good morning, Sister Julia', or 'Good morning, Sister Louisa', or 'Good morning, Sister Clara', as the case might be.

Sometime later, but not later than nine o'clock, the Beloved and his Brothers and Sisters would go down, dressed, for breakfast.

*

Much of the credit for holding Prince to the promise he made to abolish sin belongs to Louisa. Julia naturally made no mention of it to him; I shall describe, in her own words, how she felt about the matter until the thing had finally become a custom in the place. It will suffice now to say that her attitude was balanced but, I think, wistful. But it was Prince, surprisingly, who proved most difficult. While the builders were in – and that was for eighteen months or more – he never once referred to the matter, being wholly absorbed in the fascinating business of bricks and mortar.

But Louisa fretted, and so did Harriet, Clara and Agnes. They did not refer to the money they had given towards the whole project, even among themselves. They were tolerably happy with their husbands, and more than happy with the running of the little community. But Prince had promised, and his neglect to keep his word seemed almost – if such a thing had been possible a stain on his character.

But as the builders left one by one, their respective tasks completed, and as the pails and brushes disappeared from the Abode and normal life began, Louisa, especially when they gathered round the fire in the evening, again and again brought the conversation round to sin, or rather, its fortunate absence.

'How happy I am,' she would say, 'to be free from the burden of sin,' or 'I can scarcely believe that a person so humble and ignorant as myself should be among the first human beings to be without the curse of the Garden of Eden,' or remarks similar in content. She undoubtedly sounded stilted; she was, after all, only repeating parrot-wise the things she had heard in Prince's speeches. But the very artificiality of her conversation at last weaned Prince's thoughts away from his building contractors, and one day, his normal feelings asserted themselves and he saw once again that Louisa, as Bunt had said, was an attractive woman. There were several steps to be taken before the state of affairs that I have described above could become regular and accepted, among them the ceremony which Bunt devised and Prince named, the Great Manifestation. That done, Prince kept his promise to Harriet, Clara, Louisa (who was first) and Agnes (who was the most delighted), and continued to keep it until trouble clouded the serenity of the Abode.

Until then, life ran evenly for all, from breakfast to bed-time. As the brothers and sisters assembled each morning in the breakfast-room they shook hands, always according to protocol. This protocol had been devised by Prince, for he had at last found a way of preventing the four Lampeter Brethren from plaguing him with religious monologues or theological questions. He had settled their respective roles at the coming Apocalypse once and for all. He had made their positions hierarchic and cut and dried. There was no possibility of further discussion. 'Mossoo', Brother George, was given the post of the First Anointed One. His role was to gather the faithful on the day of wrath and act as an aide to Prince. The other three were appointed Angels of the Blasts of the Trumpet – the first, second and third. The ladies, not to be left out of this, were appointed Witnesses who would speak when called upon of the record of the faithful.

Having devised all this, Prince never again referred to it for the rest of his life except to appoint new members of the hierarchy when it became necessary. He merely insisted that in shaking hands, in going for walks, in sitting round the dining-room table or the fire, the gradations should be properly observed. They were. This fact engaged Prince's amused attention for some time, and he toyed with the idea of constructing a more elaborate ladder of titles. But he lost interest. He found the Great Manifestation much more to his liking, but that was probably because it was wholly devised by Sergeant Bunt.

*

The Great Manifestation was held whenever Prince chose a new bride from among his disciples to take to bed. It might, perhaps, have been more poetically named, but the title was given it by Prince himself, who was not good at such things. 'The Adullam', 'The Great Declaration', even 'The Agapemone' were not the inspired phrases one might expect from a man so versed in the Song of Solomon. The title of the present ceremony dated from the days Prince spent pacing up and down his Brighton room. There was, at that time, in his mind, the notion of some impressive manifestation of the fact that he had abolished sin, to take place once and for all time.

But the more Prince became absorbed in the Abode, its construction, its running, and its inmates, the more careless he grew of theology. We have seen how he disposed of the questions of his fellow clergymen: in all other matters connected with his principles he gradually ceased to say anything at all. By the time that the Abode was functioning smoothly and manifestations of the abolition of sin became frequent, and even customary, he could not bother to think of titles at all. The Great Manifestation was in practice not great at all; it was small in scale, and domestic in atmosphere.

A ceremony of some sort, was, of course, thought necessary; neither Prince nor Bunt wanted to repeat the mistake of the Riggses. Prince went so far as to suggest that he and say, Louisa, or Agnes or whoever was currently chosen, should wear a flower in their hair. But Sergeant Bunt pointed out that Prince would have to do the same, and an experiment in front of a mirror with a carnation quickly put that out of court. Prince then left the matter to Bunt's inventive mind, and Bunt devised the following proceedings.

Prince would name the woman of his current choice to Bunt, and Bunt would fill that fortunate lady's bedroom with flowers. The Riggses cast their shadow so far but no farther. The flowers were not carelessly plucked forest blossoms, but they were rather stiff bouquets, wired with Bunt's artistic but still soldierly hand.

The faithful gathered, by invitation, in the church after dinner, which was eaten in the Abode at the late hour of seven o'clock. Bunt, meantime, had rearranged the chairs and moved the sofa to an alcove against the south wall. The billiard table, which was too heavy to shift, was draped in a large plush table-cover of a wine-red colour, ornamented in the style of the times with heavy wool tassels. The alcove itself was set with vases of flowers, and the couch covered with a piece of gold brocade, on which rested ample cushions. These, originally plain, were later most beautifully embroidered by Harriet with the more passionate verses of the Song of Solomon, done in cross-stitch gothic lettering.

The faithful met and all shook hands, according to the hierarchic degree of each person. A tea-tray, with a kettle on a spirit stove, was wheeled in for the ladies. The gentlemen supplied themselves from the tantalus that always stood on a mahogany table under one of the stained-glass windows. The butler moved among the disciples, who were all dressed in their formal evening clothes. It was a rigid rule that, in this preliminary quarter of an hour, nothing but light topics should be discussed. The gentlemen ventured upon harmless jokes, the ladies laughed. The general air of the gathering, at least after a few minutes, was deliberately relaxed and happy, in tribute to the fact that sin had been abolished.

The butler would now come in and take away some of the lamps, but leaving one to illuminate the alcove, one by the harp which stood in a corner, and one to shine on the semicircle of disciples who were now all seated. This done, a member of the hierarchy would, without rising, give a short address, rehearsing Prince's declaration, and reminding his listeners of the closely reasoned theological basis which underlay the event they were about to witness. This speaker, it was found, could most usefully be the former husband of the bride (if there was one), for the chance to deliver a sermon usually overcame any wavering he might feel in his faith. This, at least, is what Prince told Bunt when things were originally mapped out.

Bunt now rang, from outside, a small bell mounted on the wall. He then flung open the main (or western) door, usually kept closed, and announced: 'The Beloved cometh, with his Bride'. At this point a talented disciple, Sister Ellen, who had been at Brighton, struck up a melody on the harp.

The bride was never named in the ceremony – it was scarcely necessary since everyone knew who she was – but for the purpose of seeing the proceedings more clearly in the mind's eye, it would be better to choose one specific bride out of the many that Prince honoured. Harriet suggests herself as the eldest, but she was always a little stiff and awkward, and in any case, her love for Prince and his for her quickly cooled. Clara and Agnes were frequent performers (it must be remembered that the ceremony took place whenever Prince *changed* his preference, and thus one disciple could figure in it several times), but the woman whom all considered the most satisfactory, and the most moving bride, was Louisa.

Prince and Louisa, then, would walk into the church, Louisa leaning on Prince's arm in the customary manner, not wearing a bridal dress, but nevertheless in a white gown. She wore jewels, as did Prince in his cuffs and shirt-front, he having long ago abandoned clerical dress.

The ladies and gentlemen now rose, and when the couple had come to the middle of the semicircle, the women kissed the bride on her cheek, while the men shook the Beloved's hand. The harpist continued to be seated, and to play.

Prince now took Louisa by the hand, and holding it high as if for entering upon some set dance, he led her to the couch amid the pattering of applause from the company. Prince and Louisa sat on the couch. Then Prince took Louisa in his arms and kissed her long and lovingly.

There was now a brief concert. Prince had a great dislike for serious music, but enjoyed a popular ballad. He always insisted that the bride of the moment should choose her own music, and this was played, and sung by Sister Ellen and whoever had the most suitable voice. Louisa chose ballads by Tom Moore, and for this Lewis Price had an admirable high tenor.

It cannot be said that the singing and playing was of a particular high standard. But at that time such little recitals took place in every drawing-room of the land, and that at the Abode was no worse than was usual.

The concert was short, and at its end Prince kissed the bride again amid more applause. The butler, helped by Bunt, now brought in lanterns of ornate iron-work of a sort which are nowadays seen only in porches, but which were then much in vogue for walking in the dark. The lanterns were already lit, symbolizing the flame of pure love which Prince had lit in all their hearts. Holding these lanterns the company made up a small procession, with Prince and the bride in their midst. They now accompanied the couple out of the church, into the portico and so, if it were not raining, across the lawn to one of the wings. There the nuptial pair were left. The disciples returned to the church, where the concert, in a more easy fashion, was resumed. After some more songs, there would be billiards, or conversation, or parlour games, until it was time to retire.

*

It is a pity that so well-bred a ceremony decayed as the years went by, but there is no doubt that this happened. Prince began to choose his brides not only from his intimate followers but from among those living in the dependencies. There was less formality in his bearing on the couch and more abandon in his kisses. The company, too, as it grew older, was less restrained in drinking, and the tea-tray gave way to wine for the ladies. Some scandal was caused, and the Great Manifestation became the most dubious aspect of the Abode of Love, so far as rumour and gossip were concerned. This was, perhaps, inevitable. But Sergeant Bunt's intentions had been good, and it is certain that they were kept to in the earlier years. But all institutions decay, and so did the Great Manifestation. It was extended, as time wore on, to bridegrooms other than Prince, and that was probably a major mistake. But even at its most careless, the ceremony always managed to add that touch of formality to the inmate's nuptials which, even in a sinless habitation, as Bunt rightly saw, was necessary.

Prince did not like children but, of course, they came. There was never a great number of them, but the first, which was Louisa's, was enough to set Prince a knotty theological problem. Children, in theory, are proof of man's fallen estate. They are the result of the sin committed in the Garden of Eden. How, then, could a sinless union produce children?

How, indeed? Prince never found the answer and never troubled much to look for it. He accounted for Louisa's child by saying it was a lapse of faith on her part, but he did not dogmatically press the argument. He let it be understood that children were undesirable, but that was all. When they came – it was arranged that they should be born in comfort, but in secrecy, at Bristol – they were not allowed in the church, the drawing-room, or at meals. Otherwise, they played on the lawn, ate in the nursery, and were schooled by William Cobbe, very much like children in any remote country house.

There was only one difference. Prince did not discourage visitors to the Abode, provided they were seeking after the light of truth and not vulgar sightseers. He wished them to carry away a good impression and for that reason he did not want them to be confused by the sight of two or three children playing, for instance, on the lawn. When visitors came, the children had to disappear.

After some experiments, Bunt finally hit upon an effective signal. As soon as a carriage was seen in the drive, he blew piercingly upon a bo'sun's whistle, and the children scampered for cover.

8
Julia

THERE were numerous visitors. *Murray's Handbook*, a guide-book of the times, listed the Abode as one of the principal curi-osities of that part of England, adding dramatically: 'No stranger is admitted to the Agapemone.' This was not true. A stranger had merely to put up the night in Bridgwater, send, as good manners demanded, a letter, and he would be shown over the house and grounds. The tour was confined, with great strict-ness, to the theological curiosities. Questions about Prince's wives would be discouraged, and he would not necessarily meet Prince himself. But he would be taken to the church and shown the billiard table and he would be offered a glass of wine and some biscuits.

All such visitors noted one thing: none of the brothers or sisters were ever occupied doing anything but enjoying them-selves. They strolled, they talked, they played games of the less strenuous sort, they ate long and elaborate meals, read the latest books, and did some sewing; they paid a very occasional visit to London or Bristol; and made a hobby of putting on fine clothes; they made a hobby of taking them off, too, the customs of the place being what they were; but beyond this they did nothing. Prince had designed his harem to be a place of dalliance, and nothing but dalliance. Sergeant Bunt's two years on his island had taught Prince that such a life could be satisfying for the right sort of person.

Some of the visitors went away shocked, but not in a noisy way. One thing deadened the moral judgement of that age, as, perhaps, it would do in our own. The whole of the Abode of Love, and the people in it down to the lowest domestic, breathed prosperity. The place smelt of money and success.

This was because Larkspur had been right. Prince's sinless religion had attracted sufficient of the solid core of the country to make the place a going concern. Membership of the group of the definitely, guaranteed saved was confined, as Prince had promised, to those who had been in the ballroom at Weymouth. Put under the sort of pressure which few religious leaders have found strength to resist, Prince soon broadened his recruitment. He opened a cadre of the provisionally saved – those who he felt would have been in the ballroom if they could. They were not honoured as the others were. They were never invited to the intimate gatherings in the church, unless, by chance, one of them was chosen as a Bride. But they lived happily in the de-pendencies, and there was never a vacancy there. Prince even had to provide accommodation for a fluctuating number of sup-porters and handmaidens – men and women who wished to pass a month, or a week, or a season, in the tranquil ambiance of Spaxton. All in all, he collected six hundred sworn and devoted followers, up and down the country, who placed their well-lined purses at his disposal. Even in its declining years, when Prince was old, the Abode was joined by one Hotham Maber with his four sisters, who together made a contribution of no less than £10,000. Prince rewarded Maber with a post among the Anointed Ones, but he scarcely needed the money. Prince him-self, from the day he finished the buildings, never did another stroke of work until the day he died: and he lived to the age of eighty-eight.

*

Prince's success delighted Julia. But she could not be as happy about the other aspects of the Abode. Yet she had predicted something of the sort, and she did not pretend that her hus-band's behaviour was a surprise. She thought the matter over with care, a hundred times, and she made up her mind how she would reply if anybody asked her about her feelings as Prince's only legal wife. It was a good reply; she had time to polish it in her thoughts, because nobody troubled to ask about her feelings until five years after the Abode of Love had been founded. Then Larkspur paid the place a visit. He wrote, as was required, from Bridgwater, and Julia opened the letter. Seeing his name, she felt unaccountably moved. When she saw him, she understood why. He reminded her of days with Prince before the Agape-mone had started and taken him away from her. She wrote to Larkspur, welcoming his visit, and found herself in tears as she sealed the letter.

*

In the five years that had passed since he had met Prince, Martin Larkspur had been as successful in his own way as Prince had been in his. Like Prince, he had mellowed. Unlike Prince, he had not given up working. He worked more than ever, but in a much more stately way. His fellow Directors had found it necessary to make him a Member of Parliament.

They did this because in large, expanding industrial economy there are unfortunately always some people who do not enter into the spirit of the thing. Many of these had seats in the House of Commons (to say nothing of those who sat, gloomy and im-movable, in the House of Lords) and there they contrived to harass such things as the new railways by inserting clauses in bills which would have checked the rate of expansion of the permanent way and of its promoters' pocket-books.

A seat had therefore been found for Larkspur so that he could carry his persuasive oratory into the Debating Chamber itself, and sway legislators as he had once swayed the small investor. The principles of what we should call his salesmanship did not change; but his manner, his vocabulary, his figures of speech and even his tailoring changed almost out of recognition. Where he had been voluble, he became deliberate; where he had been assertive, he learned to listen. He had found that the House of Commons could be led, but not bullied; it could be persuaded, but not swept off its feet; and he found, too, that it could be sold, as we should say, as easily as a clergyman, but one didn't have to speak so quickly or so loudly. He changed his tailor, and he changed his cook. He grew sober in appearance, and he grew fat.

He was sitting in the common-room of the small hotel at Bridgwater when Julia's invitation arrived. He was puffing a little as he wrote out a speech which he would be due to make on his return to London. He slowly pencilled the peroration:

'This great nation of ours, this England,' he wrote, 'is now the wonder and admiration of the world. Our English way of life, our comfort, our ever-expanding wealth, is the envy of mankind. I have faith, Mr Speaker, that, impelled forward by the inventive genius of our race, sustained by our habits of industry, and strengthened by that liberty which is an Englishman's proudest boast, we shall go on to greater things yet, to a prosperity as yet undreamed of, to a fullness of life that has no parallel in the long annals of mankind.' This was fine; but Larkspur spared no pains. He read it through again, and soon brought his pencil down on a weak spot. After the words 'we shall go on', he put a caret mark, and wrote above it 'under God'.

This brought his thoughts back to clergymen, and so to Prince. He opened Julia's letter, and called for a fly to take him to the Abode. During his journey to Spaxton he examined the countryside and found it as satisfactory as he had been told it was. He had heard much of Prince in London, and he had once read a description of the beauties of his retreat. Larkspur had made up his mind that he, too, when he retired, would have a similar house, in just such a beautiful setting.

Julia was walking in the drive when the fly passed the lodge gates. Larkspur recognized her, and had the driver pull up. As he dismounted he heard a shrill, naval whistling, as Bunt cleared the lawn of children.

He bent low over Julia's hand.

'Welcome, Mr Larkspur,' she said. 'You do us a great honour. I hear you have become a famous man.'

'Not so famous, madam, as your husband. I hear about him everywhere.'

His small dark eyes studied her face. It was thin, he thought, and a little drawn. She seemed to him much more tired and slow a woman than he remembered.

'Mr Prince asks me to say he will be delighted to see you, after you have gone round the Abode, Mr Larkspur. You do want to see it, don't you? Good. Then I shall be your guide. How pleasant it is to see you, again, Mr Larkspur. Henry and I have often talked of you, and that poor Indian woman. You remember her?'

'No, madam. I can't say that I do.'

'They were going to burn her alive, don't you remember, and you rescued her with a first-class ticket to Khatmandu.'

Larkspur snorted, and then suppressed what would have been a most unparliamentary guffaw.

'Yes, Mrs Prince. I remember the lucky lady.'

'I'm sorry that my husband never bought any of your shares, Mr Larkspur.'

'But he did, madam.'

'Oh,' said Julia. Then recovering herself. 'Oh yes, of course. I'd forgotten. I'm sure he must have told me. Did they . . . were they . . .?' She did not know how to finish her sentence.

'Were they . . . ah . . . worthless shares?' Larkspur finished for her. 'Is that what you were going to say?'

'Yes, Mr Larkspur. Yes, it was.'

'As it turned out, Mrs Prince, they were not. Your husband must have made quite a little money out of them by now.' He looked at the splendid house, the lawns, and the distant buildings of the dependencies. 'Quite a lot,' he said.

'Yes,' said Julia, following his glance, 'it has all been a very wonderful success,' said Julia. 'Now, we usually start with the church. Shall we go in?'

Larkspur removed his hat and together they went in by the west door.

She led him to the middle of the church and invited him, with a gesture, to look around him. The carpet, the potted palms, the fireplace and the billiard table glowed in October sunshine coming through the stained glass.

'I should explain,' said Julia, 'that it is part of our belief that everybody in the Agapemone is saved and so there is no point in holding services. However, since we had a church, we thought we would furnish it. I hope you'll agree it's in good taste. In any case, it is historically interesting. Ever since Henry VIII, the

English have been taking things out of churches. This is the first
time that anything has been put in to one. Well,' she said, pointing, 'that is the billiard table. You will certainly have heard all
about it at Bridgwater.'

Larkspur nodded, turned and gazed.

'They told me at the inn that you play billiards on Sundays,'
he said. 'On this table, I take it?'

'Yes,' said Julia. 'We also play on Mondays, Tuesdays, Wed-
nesdays, Thursdays, Fridays and Saturdays. You must understand that we don't make a *religion* of it.'

'Excellent,' said Larkspur. 'In fact, since you don't hold
services and you play billiards in church, it might be said that
you don't make a religion of religion at all.'

'A splendid way of putting it,' said Julia.

'I consider that a great step forward,' said Larkspur. 'It
removes the only thing that I have against religion, as a matter
of fact. I might become a convert you know, Mrs Prince. How,
for instance, does one become a member of your church?'

'It is rather complicated, Mr Larkspur, but it all turns on a
meeting at the Royal Hotel, Weymouth. In the ballroom,' said
Julia.

'When does that take place?'

'It took place five years ago, Mr Larkspur, and there aren't
going to be any more.'

'Dear me,' said Larkspur. 'I should find attending that meeting
even more difficult than keeping the Ten Commandments and
loving your neighbour, wouldn't I? I'm surprised that you make
the rules so difficult. Don't you have any missionaries?'

Julia smiled and shook her head.

'No missionaries?' said Larkspur. 'Certainly you should have
missionaries, at least for *Africa*,' and, his eyes sparkling with
delight, he made the sweeping gesture that had described the
map of Africa in his selling days. 'What have we in Africa?
Jungles.' He screwed up his eyes.

'Swamps,' said Julia, laughing.

'Wild beasts,' said Larkspur.

'Savages.'

'*Howling* savages,' corrected Larkspur, primly. 'Do you know, Mrs Prince, I often long to talk like that in the House. But they tell me it won't do.'

'Well, I remember that *I* was enormously impressed,' said Julia, still laughing. 'I recall telling Henry that you'd go far one day. And so you did. And now, since you're certainly the nicest sightseer we've had, let us go on with the tour.'

She led the way to another door, opened it and went out into the courtyard. The courtyard was paved and in the middle stood a fountain of Italian workmanship that threw up water from the horns of tritons. On three sides of the courtyard were stone buildings with carved pilasters. The fourth side had a balustrade and steps that led down out of sight.

Larkspur stopped. He pointed to the fountain:

'How very beautiful,' he said.

'Do you really think so?' said Julia. 'Yes, I can see that perhaps you do. I'm glad. It was made in Vicenza. I saw one like it when I was a girl and I told Henry – Mr Prince, that is – that if ever I had a garden I wanted one just like it. Then we came here. I thought he had forgotten. But one day I saw them unpacking the crates on the lawn. I think it was the happiest day of my life. It must have given Henry a great deal of trouble. I'm sorry for that. I . . .' She stopped. She turned her head away. 'Like all guides, Mr Larkspur,' she said, without looking at him, 'I'm becoming a chatterbox. Forgive me. Now I must show you the lawn.'

She led him to the balustrade and then down some steps that curved down directly to a broad stretch of grass, tightly mown and set round with clipped hedges, on which the fancy of a gardener had been at work. A lion, a horse's head, a peacock and a great fat hen had been cut from the hedge, and stood, each on its own leafy plinth, guarding the lawn. Distantly behind the green wall stood great trees, enclosing the lawn once again, as though in a vaster box. In the centre of all this, in the middle of the lawn, was a clump of evergreens, more roughly clipped into the shape of a dome standing on the grass. Here were more heads, but this time of marble. A bull thrust its neck through a hole in the bushes; a three-headed Cerberus was there with a marble collar, half-hidden in the leaves; a lion pushed out its head snarling, and puckering its brow; and lastly a satyr, man-size, struggled with the greenery and came out as far as his yellowing waist. It was very quiet.

'This is where we put the disciples who die,' said Julia.

'In that . . . that monument affair in the middle?' asked Lark-spur.

'No. Under the lawn. Just anywhere under the lawn.'

'How strange.'

'Isn't it? But the gardener insists that it's the best place and not even the Beloved dares contradict the gardener. He's a great artist, is our gardener.'

'So I can see,' said Larkspur. 'But do you have no tomb-stones?'

'Certainly not,' said Julia. 'We want to forget them as soon as possible.'

'The dead?'

'Yes.'

'In my experience,' said Larkspur, 'the people who want to do that immediately erect the biggest and most expensive monu-ment they can buy. This is a very novel cemetery. How many are buried here?'

'Two or three. Maybe four. I can't remember exactly.'

'And why do you want to forget these unfortunate two, or three, or four?' asked Larkspur.

'People in the Abode of Love do not die,' said Julia, firmly.

'But apparently they do.'

'Not if they have faith in the Beloved.'

'Oh,' said Larkspur. 'Oh yes. I begin to see. And these – these two or three or four out there – were backsliders?'

'Yes,' said Julia. 'The Beloved said that all who have faith in him would be immortal, because they were appointed to witness the Apocalypse. But there they are, dead. So they couldn't have had faith. Do you understand?'

'No,' said Larkspur. 'What do sightseers usually say?' he asked. 'Do they say they understand?'

'Yes,' said Julia. 'Such liars!'

'As for me,' said Larkspur. 'I tell you frankly that if a man had prophesied that I should have a thousand pounds, and instead of that I lost it, I would not call him a good prophet. But then I have never understood what it is to have faith.'

'Then I shall explain it,' said Julia.

'I am sure you can,' said Larkspur. 'You above all people.'

Julia did not appear to have heard him. 'I shall tell you,' she went on, 'about my uncle, Lord Porter, and the stable boy, and then you will understand the whole thing. The October sunshine is so very beautiful, let us go and sit on the seat under the bull.' They crossed the lawn. Larkspur looked for discoloured patches but finding none, admired the gardener's skill. They found a seat under the bull's head and they sat down.

*

'One of my uncles on my mother's side,' she said, 'is Lord Porter. I called him Uncle Henry and when I was a girl he was very fond of me. But I was always frightened of him because he was so big. He wasn't fat; he was big. He had a broad face, enormous shoulders and the rest of him was to match. He was known in sporting circles as the best amateur boxer of his time, and he believed in fairies.

'I don't mean he believed in fairies when he was talking to children or telling them stories – he used to say our fairy stories were all a pack of lies. I mean he believed in fairies when he was shaving himself, or drinking port, or riding to hounds, or out with his gun or talking to his bailiff. He believed in them all the time.

'It began when he was at school. He repeated a story about Oberon and Titania that his nurse had told him. I think it must have come from Shakespeare's plays, but the boys in Uncle Henry's school didn't know anything about Shakespeare, and I think the masters knew very little more. Uncle Henry was laughed at, first by the boys, and then, when the story got round, by the masters. So one day Uncle Henry stood in the middle of the quadrangle, took off his jacket, and said in a loud voice that he believed in fairies. Then he put up his fists. The eldest boy in the school, after a pause which he owed to his dignity, laughed, just once, and also took off his jacket. Uncle Henry knocked him down. He got up and said he still did not believe in fairies and Uncle Henry knocked him down again.

'I have seen schoolboys fighting and I do not suppose for one moment that it was really as simple as that. But Uncle Henry always said it was. He must have told me the story at least a dozen times, and in his story the other boy never laid a finger on Uncle, but just stood up and got knocked down. When I was a girl I was always secretly on that poor boy's side because I didn't believe in fairies myself, and it seemed to me he was standing up, or, rather, getting knocked down for the truth. But Uncle Henry won. To save what were left of his front teeth, the boy said: "Long live King Oberon and Queen Titania," and promised, in future, to say it on any and every occasion when Uncle Henry asked him to. Uncle Henry, as you can see, was something of a tyrant, even then. But he was a tyrant only in matters which he thought sacred and beyond dispute, like the existence of fairies.

'When he grew up he became the master of a great property near Exton, which he ran very well. My Uncle Henry still defended his opinions stoutly, and his favourite place for doing it was at the Taunton fair. He would go there for the cock-fighting, of which he was passionately fond, and for a glass or two with his cock-fighting cronies. When they had had enough of their sport and perhaps too much of their liquor, they would take Uncle Henry to one of the prize-fighters' booths and there Uncle Henry would take off his jacket and say: "I believe in King Oberon and Queen Titania and I will knock down any man of my size and weight or over who says they don't exist." Since everybody knew he was Lord Porter, nobody would step up to fight until he would say: "and I have twenty golden guineas to back my opinion." This made it a prize-fight and one by one the yokels would come up and try to knock my uncle down and win the golden guineas, but none of them ever managed it.

'In his own house he was popular. Although he was so big and powerful he had an easy temper, and he was liked by his servants and farm hands, who quickly learned (without, I think, any of them being knocked down) to believe in fairies. They were grateful to them, for the Little People were the cause of Uncle Henry's good temper.

'He was convinced that everything that mortals did was supervised and sometimes interfered with by these invisible beings. When things went wrong it was all their doing, and the thing to find out, according to Uncle Henry, was why they did it. Sometimes it would be for pure sport – Uncle Henry understood sporting fairies very well – but sometimes it would be a punishment, inflicted on the orders of His Diminutive Majesty himself, for some disrespect, or neglect. When things went well, it was equally the fairies that had to be thanked. Since Uncle Henry believed that fairies were all-powerful, even over the weather, his theory covered every conceivable happening. Therefore, he was quite happy, like a Mohammedan resigning himself to the will of Allah.

'You would have thought that the servants would have taken advantage of this state of affairs, but they didn't, at least so far as I know. Some of the younger ones may have pocketed a spoon or two, but on the whole they found it so useful to blame all their mistakes on the fairies, and so get themselves a quiet life, that they didn't wish to disturb the happy state of affairs by doing anything too blatant. Besides, they must have had misgivings, at times, especially at breakfast. When my Uncle Henry would come down, perhaps after a heavy night with his sporting friends, and lumber, growling, among the covers on the sideboard, looking as big as a rhinoceros and just as dangerous, it was difficult to believe that this enormous man was sure he had sprites dancing all around him. His servants encouraged his faith: but they were careful not to test it too far.

'They had one special way of encouraging it. One day a wise woman who lived alone on the moors told him that he should always leave a platter of milk outside his house at night together with any other dainties he might choose. It was an act of courtesy to the fairy kingdom, and its inhabitants would come and drink and eat each night, just to give Uncle Henry plain proof that they really existed.

'My uncle was greatly taken with this, and immediately it was dusk, set out some saucers with milk, and one with claret, for it was one of his firmest articles of belief that the fairies, down to the lowest, were gentlefolk.

'Early the next morning, the servants were thoroughly alarmed to hear my uncle cursing loudly and horribly on the door-step. They scrambled out of bed – those who were still abed – and came running. They found my uncle bellowing by the saucers. "It's been drunk," he was roaring, and much else besides that is not fit to repeat. They saw that the milk had indeed been drunk, but the claret had not. This had roused my uncle's suspicions, and it was not long before he had found the tracks of a cat. The terrible noise which had woken the house had been my uncle saying what he would do to the cat if he caught him. Now I suppose cats all over the countryside have drunk the milk that superstitious old women put out on their door-steps, and nobody has minded, or noticed. But my uncle's faith was deeper, and he did.

'After everybody in the house had passed a very bad morning, the carpenter came up with an ingenious notion which he was instantly set to carry out. He made a wire cage with a small door which could be locked. The food was to be put inside, the door locked, and the key hung on a hook on the door jamb, conveniently for fairy fingers to find. That night all the servants slept peacefully in their beds, except (so he has told me) the butler. He woke at three o'clock in the morning, and in that awful clear-headedness which we all get at that hour in the morning, saw something they had all overlooked. Trembling from fright at his narrow escape, he crept downstairs, opened the cage, and drank both the milk and the claret. He then locked the cage neatly again, and went back to bed, feeling reassured, but I should think, a little queasy. The next morning my Uncle Henry was found at the cage, beaming mightily. The house, from that day onwards, ran smoothly and tranquilly. Uncle Henry would often take me with him to fill the cage, and he never failed to impress on me that when I grew up and heard people criticize his beliefs, since I was a girl and could not offer to knock them down (which was the best way), I was to tell them the story of the cage and how it was locked every night, and how the victuals were consumed.

'But the years passed and the butler grew older. He was less and less inclined to get out of bed in the middle of the night. He deputed his task to a footman (who merely threw the stuff into the bushes) and when the footman got tired of it, the butler came to a sensible arrangement with the grooms. Since they were accustomed to getting up very early to exercise the horses and since they were as dependent as anybody on the fairies for a quiet life, theirs became the task of emptying the cage in good time. This they did, but it was inevitable that such a task should filter down to the youngest employee of all, until the time came when the duty fell on a youthful and very indolent stable-boy called Harry.

'Harry obeyed his orders for a few days, but one cold winter's morning he put his head out of the blankets and put it back quickly again, to have just five more minutes in bed. Well, he fell asleep again and did not wake up until it was much too late. My Uncle Henry had gone down to inspect the cage as he always did, and, of course, he found that the fairies were angry with him.

'The butler told me that in all the years that he'd served my uncle, he'd never seen him so sunk in black gloom as he saw him all the morning. My uncle had made up his mind that he had offended the fairies in some really gross way, and the more he tried to think what he had done, the gloomier he grew.

'His temper became so bad that when the butler served him his food on unwarmed plates at supper, he quarrelled with the poor man, a thing he had never done before. The butler, in tears, tried to excuse himself, and in describing how the whole household was upset, he let slip the name of Harry, the stable-boy.

'My uncle immediately grew calmer. He asked the butler to explain what he meant. The butler knew his master; and he knew that there would be no use in trying to dodge the issue. He made a clean breast of the whole thing. He told my uncle how they had conspired to empty the cage, with no other purpose than to please him, and how Harry had let them down.

'My uncle got straight up from the table, called for his great-coat, and went out to the stables. He asked to see Harry. The trembling boy was produced. My uncle, towering over him, asked him if it was true that he had been told to empty the cage, and that he had forgotten to do it. Harry, thinking that he would be knocked down at any moment, said that it was quite true, and that when he had woken up, the early morning had been so cold that he had gone back to bed and gone to sleep again, quite by mistake. My uncle looked very serious. He said: "Harry, it is a very, very bad thing to neglect to do your duty. You don't understand that now because you are too young, but you will understand when you grow up. Now I want you to promise me that you will get up every morning for the next month and for as long after that as you are told, and clear the cage according to the butler's instructions. If you are a good boy for one month, which will be thirty days, I shall give you thirty shillings." Harry, who could not believe his ears, hurriedly prom- ised, and Uncle Henry left the stables. On the way back to the house, so the butler told me, he said: "He's certainly a lazy little devil, but, by God, it was certainly very cold this morning." And he said nothing more at all.

'Well, as you may imagine, Harry took good care to earn his reward. But what astonished the butler and everybody else in the house, was that next morning, and for every morning after that Uncle Henry came down, just as usual, and went to the cage to see if the fairies had drunk up his gift. And when he found that they had, he beamed, as he had always done, and he was happy and contented for the rest of the day. What was more, he never failed to take visitors to the cage, and explain how it was locked every night, and how every morning he found that the fairies had come and drunk up every drop of the milk and the claret. On market days, after cock-fighting, he would go to the prize-fighters' booths, as he had always done, take off his jacket and say: "I believe in King Oberon and Queen Titania and I will knock down any man of my size and weight who says they don't exist, and I have twenty golden guineas to back my opinion." He never once mentioned Harry, until the end of his life. And so,' said Julia, looking up, 'when things happen here that I don't understand or . . .' She paused. 'Things that I don't very much like,' she went on, 'I think of my uncle.'

She looked across the lawn. 'Well, now,' she said. 'I have been gossiping and I have delayed you. Here comes my husband. He must be wondering what has happened to you all this time.'

*

When Larkspur left the Abode, he pressed Julia's hand and said that he greatly admired her and sincerely hoped he would see her again. But he did not. Julia fell seriously ill a few days later. When it became clear that she had no hope of recovering, Prince sat by her bed day and night. They would sometimes talk a little, although she was very weak. When they did, it was always of the days before they had come to Spaxton.

One night, at eleven o'clock, when she had been sleeping fitfully, she suddenly woke and called out for Prince. He was at her bedside, and he took her hand.

'Henry,' she said. 'I am going to die.'

Henry, unable to speak because of his tears, pressed her hand. She closed her eyes, shook her head impatiently as she remembered that to die was wrong and that she should not do it.

Then suddenly she felt her last strength ebbing away. She opened her eyes and looked at her husband for the last time.

'Henry,' she whispered, 'I am so sorry . . . so very sorry,' and she died.

9
Epilogue

WITH Julia's death, the shadows began to gather round the Abode. Prince, his theology forgotten, was stricken with grief. When he recovered, he was much changed. He was slower in his movements, and his face was greatly aged. He seemed to care little for the house and his disciples, and he became solitary. Then a year later his spirits revived, but not in a way that gave much pleasure to the others. He began to take as brides several young girls who, on the thinnest of pretexts, he declared were members of the community, bringing them back from mysterious and secret journeys to Bristol. Then he fell in love with a Miss Paterson, the daughter of a widow who was a genuine, and paying, adherent. A Manifestation was held, as usual, but Prince's behaviour at it was very coarse. His formal kiss was an unbridled pawing affair that shocked Harriet very deeply.

Afterwards Harriet protested. The basis of her protest was curious. She objected that Prince's behaviour was no longer *respectable*, and that she, a respectable woman, would not tolerate it. She left, with her husband. Prince gave her back her money. He seemed, when he did it, barely to know who she was.

Harriet was the second to go. Poor Agnes, spurned by her indifferent husband and now ignored by the infatuated Prince, had left before. She, too, was given her money. Prince was now a rich man and paying back his capital presented him with no difficulty at all.

There were no more desertions, and there were even, as we have seen, some recruits. But the great days of the Abode were over, and Prince sank rapidly into his prolonged old age.

*

He did not lack company. There was Bunt, an old man now but

still able to go about his duties. There was also Larkspur, for he had retired, as he had planned, to a property within a mile or so of the Abode of Love. He drove over frequently to see Prince, to keep him company, for he, never having married, had none himself.

One day he and Prince were sitting by the fire in the church and Bunt was seeing that they were both comfortable, when Larkspur said:

'Prince, you've led a fine life. A lovely house, money, and all the women you have ever wanted. What do you think of it all?'

'All?' said Prince. 'You mean what do I think about the women. That's it, isn't it? That's what they all ask.'

'Well, yes,' said Larkspur. 'Yes. The women.'

'Ask Bunt,' said Prince. Then raising his voice querulously, 'Bunt! Stop fussing about, Bunt, and sit down. Larkspur wants to know what I think about my women. Tell him your story, Bunt. Tell him.'

Bunt sat down.

'Well, it's just something I heard in Alexandria when I was at sea, twenty, oh, it must be thirty, thirty-five years ago, now . . .'

'Get on, get on, Bunt,' said Prince.

'It's nothing much to tell, Mr Larkspur,' said Bunt, 'but it's always taken Mr Prince's fancy. There was a man in Alexandria who had a lot to do with the ladies, sir, in the way of business, and he once told me the wisest thing he ever heard about them. It seems that there was a rich pasha in Cairo, if pasha's the right word, sir, who built himself a palace by the Nile, and, if you'll forgive the phrase, sir, fair stocked it with ladies that had taken his fancy. Quite a lifetime's work he made of it, or hobby, if you prefer the word. He had a pretty wide fancy, too, by all accounts, and he had upwards of three hundred lady friends under his roof, and the man who told me about it had helped him in making what you might call his collection, sir. Well, Mr Larkspur, this pasha considered himself a fortunate man as well he might, but somehow he always felt he'd missed something, sir;

what it was he didn't know, but he knew he wasn't happy like he'd aimed to be. Then one evening, he was sitting on his balcony which overlooked the Nile, sir, when he heard a young man sighing to himself and weeping; sir, these Egyptians being very emotional people, sir, as I know from my own experience, me having been three, no, it must be four times to Alexandria not counting – '

'Bunt,' said Prince, testily, 'do get *on*.'

'Yes, sir. Well, this young man gave over sighing after a bit, and then said a girl's name aloud, so the pasha knew that his trouble was over a lady, sir, as it so often is. Then this young man began singing to himself, and fitting words to the tune, sir, as these Egyptians do, at least the educated ones, and this young man was very educated, like Mr Prince and yourself, sir, only he made up poetry: just two lines, sir, what they call a gazelle but why I cannot say, sir, it being an unlikely sort of name. At any rate when the pasha heard this particular gazelle, he struck his forehead and said: "That's it; that is what I have been missing – the true pleasure of love, the only real pleasure of love. What a fool I've been. *What* a fool!" And from that day onwards, sir, he wasn't a bit interested in all the three hundred ladies he had collected, not one bit.'

Bunt stopped and gazed into the dying fire.

'He was quite right, too,' said Prince. 'Quite right. It's the only way that you can have anything to do with women and not be sorry.' He, too, fell silent and stared into the fire.

'Well,' said Larkspur. 'What *was* it that the young man sang?'

Bunt started. 'Oh, didn't I tell you, sir?' he said. 'I'm very sorry. The young man sang, sir, "*The girl on the other side of the river has a beautiful backside; but I have no boat,*" if you'll excuse the quotation, sir.'

Prince nodded his white head sagely two or three times.

'No boat,' he said. 'Lucky fellow.' He sighed. Then turning to Bunt he said: 'Bunt, what a chatterbox you are. While you've been talking the fire's nearly gone out. Put some logs on it, will you, Bunt? It's getting very chilly.'

MORE ABOUT PENGUINS

For further information about books available from Penguins in India write to Penguin Books (India) Ltd, B4/246, Safdarjung Enclave, New Delhi 110 029.

In the UK: For a complete list of books available from Penguins in the United Kingdom write to Dept. EP, Penguin Books Ltd, Harmondsworth, Middlesex UB7 0DA.

In the U.S.A.: For a complete list of books available from Penguins in the United States write to Dept. DG, Penguin Books, 299 Murray Hill Parkway, East Rutherford, New Jersey 07073.

In Canada: For a complete list of books available from Penguins in Canada write to Penguin Books Canada Ltd, 2801 John Street, Markham, Ontario L3R 1B4.

In Australia: For a complete list of books available from Penguins in Australia write to the Marketing Department, Penguin Books Australia Ltd, P.O. Box 257, Ringwood, Victoria 3134.

In New Zealand: For a complete list of books available from Penguins in New Zealand write to the Marketing Department, Penguin Books (N.Z.) Ltd, Private Bag, Takapuna, Auckland 9.

THE NIGHT TRAIN AT DEOLI
AND OTHER STORIES
Ruskin Bond

The best of a lifetime of stories from a short story writer of rare distinction. Ruskin Bond's stories are predominantly set in the beautiful hill country of Garhwal where he has made his home for the last twenty-five years. Some of these stories present people who, consciously or otherwise, need each other: people in love or in need of love, the awkward adolescent and the timid lover. Some are gently satirical studies about village and small-town braggarts and petty officials. Several others mourn the gradual erosion of the beauty of the hills with the coming of the steel and dust and worries of modern civilization. All the stories are rewarding for their compassionate portrayal of love, loss, accomplishment, pain and struggle.

'There is something about most of the stories that touch the deepest chord of the reader's heart...'

—*Financial Express*

THE DEVIL'S WIND: NANA SAHEB'S STORY
Manohar Malgonkar

Nana Saheb was arguably India's greatest hero in the country's early battles against the British. This novel, by one of India's finest writers, brings alive the sequence of events that led the adopted son of the Maratha Peshwa Bajirao II to take on the British in the Great Revolt of 1857.

'A fascinating novel'—*The Sunday Times*

'A tragic and tremendous story'—*Pearl S. Buck*

'(Malgonkar writes) compellingly'—*Paul Scott*

NUDE BEFORE GOD
Shiv K. Kumar

Just as Ramkrishna, a painter, is convinced there is far more to life than portraits of fat industrialists and buxom nudes, he is murdered. But his problems don't end there. Under a special dispensation granted by Yama, the Lord of Death, he is able to spy on those he left behind—his unfaithful wife, her murderous lover, his unhappy dog, his jealous collegues.... Just when their actions are beginning to really get to him the plot takes a wholly unexpected twist.

'A most amusing book on a daring subject'—*Graham Greene*

THE ROOM ON THE ROOF
Ruskin Bond

Rusty, a sixteen-year-old Anglo-Indian boy, is dissatisfied with life in the declining European community at Dehra Dun. So he runs away from home to live with Indian friends who introduce him, much to his delight, to the dream bright world of *bazaar* life, Hindu festivals and a way of being that seems utterly enchanting. Rusty is hooked at once by all this and is forever lost to the prim proprieties of the European community.

'Mr Bond is a writer of great gifts'
—*The New Statesman*

'Like an Indian bazaar itself, the book is filled with the smells, sights, sounds, confusion and subtle organization of ordinary Indian life'
—'Santha Rama Rau in the *New York Times Book Review*

Winner of the John Llewellyn Rhys Memorial Prize

A DEATH IN DELHI :
Modern Hindi Short Stories
Translated & Edited by
Gordon C. Roadarmel

A collection of brilliant new stories from the writers who have revolutionized Hindi literature over the past forty years. The short stories in this volume take up from where Premchand (the greatest writer Hindi has ever produced) and his immediate successors left off and offer the reader an excellent and entertaining introduction to the diversity and richness that the modern short story at its best can offer. Among the writers represented are Nirmal Verma, Krishna Baldev Vaid, Shekhar Joshi Phanishwarnath 'Renu', Gyanranjan and Mohan Rakesh.

'By far the best collection of recent Hindi short stories to have appeared in English'.
—*David Rubin*